Chance Had Never In His Life Been Aroused By The Sight Of A Pregnant Woman.

But Kristen standing in front of the mirror with the pillow stuffed under her shirt, the sight of her slender fingers splayed along the sides of her pretend belly, had excited the hell out of him. She'd looked so beautiful, so feminine, so…pregnant with his child.

How would Kristen look six months from now if she did have his baby nestled safely inside of her?

True, he hadn't envisioned himself with a city gal like Kristen. However, suddenly the thought of staying married to Kristen wasn't such an unpleasant idea. Unlike his own mother, he was determined to be a good parent and be there for his kids. And the way he saw it, he and Kristen would be married for nine more months if she *was* pregnant.

The least they could do would be to give the whole thing a damned good shot for the baby's sake.…

Dear Reader,

Twenty years ago in May, the first Silhouette romance was published, and in 2000 we're celebrating our 20th anniversary all year long! Celebrate with us—and start with six powerful, passionate, provocative love stories from Silhouette Desire.

Elizabeth Bevarly offers a MAN OF THE MONTH so tempting that we decided to call it *Dr. Irresistible!* Enjoy this sexy tale about a single-mom nurse who enlists a handsome doctor to pose as her husband at her tenth high school reunion. The wonderful miniseries LONE STAR FAMILIES: THE LOGANS, by bestselling author Leanne Banks, continues with *Expecting His Child,* a sensual romance about a woman carrying the child of her family's nemesis after a stolen night of passion.

Ever-talented Cindy Gerard returns to Desire with *In His Loving Arms,* in which a pregnant widow is reunited with the man who's haunted her dreams for seven years. Sheikhs abound in Alexandra Sellers' *Sheikh's Honor,* a new addition to her dramatic miniseries SONS OF THE DESERT. The Desire theme promotion, THE BABY BANK, about women who find love unexpectedly when seeking sperm donors, continues with Metsy Hingle's *The Baby Bonus.* And newcomer Kathie DeNosky makes her Desire debut with *Did You Say Married?!,* in which the heroine wakes up in Vegas next to a sexy cowboy who turns out to be her newly wed husband.

What a lineup! So this May, for Mother's Day, why not treat your mom—and yourself—to all six of these highly sensual and emotional love stories from Silhouette Desire!

Enjoy!

Joan Marlow Golan

Joan Marlow Golan
Senior Editor, Silhouette Desire

Please address questions and book requests to:
Silhouette Reader Service
U.S.: 3010 Walden Ave., P.O. Box 1325, Buffalo, NY 14269
Canadian: P.O. Box 609, Fort Erie, Ont. L2A 5X3

Did You Say Married?!

KATHIE DeNOSKY

Silhouette® Desire®

Published by Silhouette Books

America's Publisher of Contemporary Romance

To Charlie, Bryan, David and Angie,
for always believing in me.
To Margie and Dorothy, for the encouragement.

And a special thanks to
Ginny, Rox, Janet, Belinda, Wayne,
Roxanne and Micqui.
I couldn't have done it without you.

 SILHOUETTE BOOKS

ISBN 0-373-76296-8

DID YOU SAY MARRIED?!

Visit Silhouette at www.eHarlequin.com

Printed in U.S.A.

KATHIE DeNOSKY

lives in deep Southern Illinois with her husband, Charlie, and their three children. She began reading romances as a teenager, but it wasn't until her youngest child started school that she decided to seriously consider writing one. A former Folk Art and Decorative Painting instructor, she loves painting pictures with words now, instead of a paintbrush. You can write to Kathie at P.O. Box 2064, Herrin, Illinois 62948.

IT'S OUR 20th ANNIVERSARY!
We'll be celebrating all year,
Continuing with these fabulous titles,
On sale in May 2000.

Romance

#1444 Mercenary's Woman
Diana Palmer

#1445 Too Hard To Handle
Rita Rainville

#1446 A Royal Mission
Elizabeth August

#1447 Tall, Strong & Cool Under Fire
Marie Ferrarella

#1448 Hannah Gets a Husband
Julianna Morris

#1449 Her Sister's Child
Lilian Darcy

Desire

#1291 Dr. Irresistible
Elizabeth Bevarly

#1292 Expecting His Child
Leanne Banks

#1293 In His Loving Arms
Cindy Gerard

#1294 Sheikh's Honor
Alexandra Sellers

#1295 The Baby Bonus
Metsy Hingle

#1296 Did You Say Married?!
Kathie DeNosky

Intimate Moments

#1003 Rogue's Reform
Marilyn Pappano

#1004 The Cowboy's Hidden Agenda
Kathleen Creighton

#1005 In a Heartbeat
Carla Cassidy

#1006 Anything for Her Marriage
Karen Templeton

#1007 Every Little Thing
Linda Winstead Jones

#1008 Remember the Night
Linda Castillo

Special Edition

#1321 The Kincaid Bride
Jackie Merritt

#1322 The Millionaire She Married
Christine Rimmer

#1323 Warrior's Embrace
Peggy Webb

#1324 The Sheik's Arranged Marriage
Susan Mallery

#1325 Sullivan's Child
Gail Link

#1326 Wild Mustang
Jane Toombs

One

Eyes still closed to prolong the dream, Chance Warren fantasized about sliding his callused palm up the satiny, smooth skin of a woman's flat stomach. His hand closed around the firm roundness of a small, perfect breast, and he smiled when the tip beaded in anticipation of his further attention.

He'd had realistic dreams before. What man hadn't? But not even when he'd been a teenager, with more hormones than good sense, had he spent an entire night dreaming the same fantasy again and again. And about the most alluring woman imaginable.

His creative mind had even supplied his vision with a name. A sweet, sexy name he'd called over and over while they'd pleasured each other throughout the night.

Christie? Crystal?

Kristen.

His groin tightened and he pressed his lips to his dream woman's bare shoulder.

Kristen. Soft, loving and capable of setting a man on fire with her hot passion.

A frown creased his forehead. He knew only one woman with that name. Kristen Lassiter. The auburn-haired ice maiden of the Dallas elite. A city gal he had about as much in common with as a politician had with the truth.

She traveled in an entirely different circle than he did. She spent her time attending charity functions and making the headlines of the society page, while he worked his butt off building his rodeo company into the best in the country. Banquets, like the one he'd attended last night, were the only occasions he ever saw her. In fact, Chance couldn't remember them ever being formally introduced. Not that it mattered. He didn't have time for a relationship with her or any other woman in his life. But it still seemed odd that he'd dream about making love to her all night.

He opened one eye to a shaft of sunlight streaming through a parting in the hotel room drapes. Pain shot through his head and he swallowed hard against the cotton coating his mouth and throat.

Why had he let his friends convince him that toasting his success with a beer just wasn't the same as toasting with champagne? The damned stuff always gave him a god-awful headache. And it only took a couple of glasses to give him a blank spot as to how much fun he'd had the night before.

Something—no, *someone* stirred beside him, and Chance gingerly turned his head. When his gaze clashed with the greenest eyes he'd ever seen, his brows shot up and he sucked in a sharp breath. Despite the pain stabbing at his brain, his own eyes widened in disbelief and the breath lodged in his lungs.

The woman beside him—his dream woman—wasn't a dream at all. The female he'd dreamed of loving throughout the night, the one whose breast he still held—he quickly snatched his hand away—was very real and none other than the ice maiden of high society, Kristen Lassiter.

They stared at each other for a long moment before Chance watched her open her mouth, scream at the top of her lungs and, taking the sheet with her, scramble from the bed.

Her shrill cry vibrated through his head. He felt his skull just might explode. "Lady, do that again and I won't be responsible for my actions," he warned, pressing his palms against his temples to hold his brains inside.

"What are you doing in my bed?" she demanded, wrapping herself in the sheet.

Chance glanced around. "I think you'd better take stock of where you are, Ms. Lassiter," he whispered. Even that hurt his head. "This is my room."

Her gaze swept the room. "But how—"

"Will you lower your voice?" He sat up and eased his legs over the side of the bed. Propping his elbows on his knees, he cradled his throbbing head in his hands. "Every time you open your mouth, it feels like there's a jackhammer chipping away at my brain."

"Well, excuse me, Mr. Warren," she said sarcastically. "I happen to be upset."

He slowly raised his head to meet her disturbed gaze. "Could you be a little quieter about it?"

"Only if you cover yourself." Her cheeks reddened. "This is embarrassing enough as it is."

He reached for the blanket, but the apologetic smile he intended to give her turned to a grimace. The facial movement made his hair follicles ache.

"I think we've gone way beyond—"

"Don't say it," she warned, sniffling.

When she glanced toward the door, Chance watched her close her eyes, then open them as if hoping the sight before her would disappear. A jumble of his and her garments trailed all the way across the room. A black sequined dress and silver pumps, along with his western-cut tuxedo jacket, shirt and boots, lay in a tangled heap just inside the door. A few feet away, a black satin slip peeked from beneath his tailored slacks. On the far side of the bed, and appearing to have been discarded in great haste, lacy black panties, garter belt and hose lay atop his white cotton briefs.

He watched her zero in on his new hat band, the sight stopping her cold. She gingerly picked up the Resistol to remove her wispy bra from the crown.

"Do you remember what happened last night?" he asked.

She dropped his hat as if she'd touched something repulsive. "Of course I do. I attended the Professional Bull Riders awards banquet and then...then..."

"Me, neither." Chance massaged his temples. "The last thing I remember I was talking to some reporter from the *Rodeo Review* about Gray Ghost being named Bucking Bull of the Year. Somebody shoved another glass of champagne into my hand and..." Trying to think, he paused. "After that I draw a blank."

When Kristen sniffed again, Chance glanced up. He hoped like hell she didn't turn on the waterworks. Teary

females made him about as nervous as a bull calf at cas-
trating time.

"You're not going to cry, are you?"

She gave him a look that sent the room temperature
down by at least ten degrees. "I have a cold."

Return of Ms. Deep Freeze, Chance thought ruefully.
He watched her gather the rest of her clothes, then walk
into the bathroom and shut the door with a resounding
thud. The sound made his head throb. He tried not to
think at all while he waited for the pain to subside. There
would be plenty of time on the long drive home to analyze the contrast between the sultry fantasy of night and
the chilling reality of morning.

In what seemed record time, Kristen emerged from the
bathroom fully dressed.

Her clothes were as elegant as ever, her auburn hair
styled to perfection and her posture regally perfect. But
no matter what she wore or how she carried herself, she
couldn't erase that well-loved look. Eyes softened by ful-
filled desire and the tiny love mark on the side of her
elegant neck couldn't lie.

Satisfaction and a tinge of regret coursed through
Chance. He was responsible for her look of fulfillment.
He just wished like hell he could remember more of what
they'd shared.

"Are we in the Mirage?" Kristen asked, walking to
the door.

"MGM Grand." Careful to hold the blanket in place,
Chance rose from the bed. "I'm not sure what morning-
after protocol applies in this situation, but—"

"It's obvious neither one of us remembers how we
got to this point," Kristen interrupted. She opened the
door. "I think the less said about the matter, the better
off we'll both be. Goodbye, Mr. Warren."

Chance watched the door close with a quiet click. He felt as if he'd just been dismissed as a minor inconvenience, a mistake that could be quickly and completely forgotten.

"Well, what the hell did you expect, Warren?" he muttered, throwing the blanket aside and heading for the shower. "The lady got tipsy and fell out of her ivory tower for a night. What made you think she wouldn't break her pretty little neck climbing back up there in the light of day?"

Half an hour later, Chance put his tux in a garment bag, stuffed the rest of his clothes into his duffel, then checked his camera case to make sure the exposed rolls of film hadn't been misplaced. He couldn't wait to get on the road. It had been more than two weeks since he'd seen his niece and nephew, and with Halloween only a week away, he wanted to fulfill his promise of helping them carve a pumpkin.

As he turned to gather his wallet and loose change from the dresser, a nagging sensation deep in his gut unsettled him. He had the distinct impression he'd forgotten something very important. But he'd checked the room twice, and for the life of him, he couldn't figure out what it might be.

When he patted his front jeans pockets, his gaze zeroed in on the garment bag hanging in the closet and a smile lifted the corners of his mouth. He must have left the polished plume agate he always carried in his tux. He'd found the unusual little stone in West Texas about five years ago and he'd had good luck ever since. No way would he set foot outside the hotel room without it.

Confident that he'd solved the mystery, he slid the zipper down and searched the jacket. When he removed the stone, a parchment envelope fluttered to the floor.

Bending to retrieve it, he pocketed his lucky agate, then removed the official-looking document from the envelope and scanned the information.

As he stared in disbelief, his heart pounded hard against his rib cage. Certain key elements jumped off the page at him.

Chance T. Warren.

Kristen M. Lassiter.

United in Holy Matrimony.

"What the hell?"

Shaking his head, Chance walked to the phone and dialed the number of the chapel listed on the back of the envelope. A woman identifying herself as Shirley answered on the second ring. "I'd like to check on a marriage ceremony performed last night," he said.

"Names, please?"

"Warren and Lassiter."

He waited while Shirley put him on hold. This phony certificate had to be some kind of practical joke. His head wrangler, Zach Davis, and some of Chance's other friends had probably gotten together and set up the whole thing.

He grinned when he thought of evening the score. He'd get some little gal at the Bucket of Suds to—

"Is this Mr. Warren?"

The hair on the back of his neck stood straight up. He hadn't identified himself as the Warren half of the couple. There was only one way the woman would know. "Yes."

"Congratulations and thank you for choosing our chapel, Mr. Warren," Shirley said, her voice way too cheerful to suit him.

Chance opened his mouth, but at the moment, words

were beyond his capabilities. A strangled sound escaped from deep in his throat.

"Mr. Warren? Are you all right?"

Hell, no!

"Uh...er, yes," he finally managed to say, his voice cracking like that of a boy who'd just entered puberty.

"I'm very glad you called." The woman giggled. "It seems you and your bride were in such a hurry to start your life together, you forgot to take your wedding video. Would you like it sent to your hotel?"

"I'll...uh...that would be fine." Dazed, he told Shirley to send it to the Mirage—the hotel Kristen had mentioned—then hung up.

The sound of the broken connection galvanized him into action, and grabbing his bags, Chance headed for the door. He had to talk to Kristen. If her speedy escape from his room had been any indication, she wouldn't hang around Vegas and risk running into him again. Besides, some things just couldn't be discussed over the phone. He'd stake his reputation that she knew even less about their nuptials than he did.

Kristen's hand shook and she tried for the third time to fit the key card into the slot on her hotel room door. "Come on. Open up."

When the lock finally cooperated, she hurried inside and, removing her clothes as she crossed the room, made a beeline for the shower.

Turning on the water, she moaned. "How could you sleep with the man, Kristen?"

Beneath the warm spray, she finally let the sophisticated facade melt away and the tears flow. Humiliation and regret caused twin rivulets to mingle with the water streaming down her cheeks.

One minute she'd been at the banquet thinking how her decision not to marry Spencer Dirkson would upset her father. The next she'd awakened in the arms of the very man Mike—she hadn't called him "Dad" in years—had warned her to steer clear of. A man he didn't even want her speaking to. Ever.

Kristen's chest tightened when she thought of Mike Lassiter. For once in her life, she'd like to do something to win her father's love and approval, to be more than a major disappointment to him. But a stupid stunt like she'd pulled last night would only serve to widen the gulf between them.

Sobs racked her body, and when a wave of dizziness made her sway, she leaned her head against the tiled wall. She felt terrible. And not just emotionally.

Instead of washing away her remorse, crying only aggravated the head cold she'd fought for the past week. Now she had another sinus headache to contend with, as well as the embarrassment of spending the night with a virtual stranger.

Toweling herself dry, she threw on the hotel's complimentary bathrobe, then rummaged through her cosmetics case for the capsules her doctor had prescribed. What had she done with them? She'd taken one last night before going to the banquet....

As she looked at herself in the mirror, Kristen's eyes grew round.

At dinner, she'd ordered mineral water. Unable to taste anything, she'd drunk most of it before realizing the waiter had brought white wine. Could the wine, mixed with cold medication, explain last night being a complete blank?

"Maybe nothing happened."

Get real, Kristen.

Chance Warren didn't look the type to take a vow of celibacy. And the unfamiliar little aches she'd experienced since awakening in his arms supported that fact.

Devilishly handsome, he had enough charm to talk the birds right out of the trees. And that didn't even take into consideration his killer smile and devastating eyes. Have mercy! A woman could lose every ounce of sense she'd ever possessed when caught in his hypnotic blue gaze.

Tall, broad-shouldered and damnably sexy in a pair of jeans and western-cut shirt, Chance Warren was every woman's dream. At least every woman Kristen knew.

A heaviness settled low in her stomach when she recalled the feel of his hand caressing her breast, the strength of his arousal pressed against her thigh. She moaned at the memory of his nude body stretched across the bed.

How on earth would she ever be able to face him again without remembering his wide shoulders, the ripples of corded muscle covering his chest and stomach, the heaviness of his...

Embarrassment burned her cheeks, and shaking her head to chase away the image, Kristen hurried into the next room. She had to leave Las Vegas as soon as possible. She wanted to put as much distance as possible between herself and Chance. There was no way she wanted to risk running into him again. At least not for a while.

Jerking clothes from the hangers in the closet and scooping underwear from the dresser drawers, Kristen stuffed the garments into her suitcase. But at the sudden, unexpected sound of someone pounding on the door, she sent a second armful of lacy underwear flying in all directions.

"Kristen, open up! We have to talk."

Even before she looked through the peephole she knew it had to be Chance. She'd remember his sexy Texas drawl for the rest of her life. But why couldn't he leave well enough alone? Hadn't she suffered enough humiliation for one day?

"Go away," she shouted back. "There's nothing to discuss."

"Yes, there is," he insisted. "Now, if you don't open this door by the time I count to three, I swear I'll break it down."

"You wouldn't dare."

"Stand back and watch me, sweetheart."

Kristen bit her lower lip. He sounded deadly serious, and she had no doubt he'd follow through on his threat.

"One…two…"

"Okay. Just stop shouting."

Her trembling fingers fumbled with the locks. When she finally released the dead bolt and started to open the door, Chance shouldered his way into the room.

"How did you get up here?" she demanded. "Security—"

He waved a piece of parchment at her. "Didn't say a word once I showed them this."

"I don't know what that is or why you think we need to discuss—"

"Once you take a look at it, you'll have a fair idea," he interrupted, shoving it into her hands.

Kristen watched him remove his hat and run an agitated hand through his dark blond hair. He jammed it back on his head. A muscle along his tanned, clean-shaven jaw worked while he waited.

"What is this?" she asked.

"Just read it."

She opened the folded paper and scanned the document. Her eyes widened. "Is this some kind of joke?"

His expression grim, he shook his head. "I called the chapel and verified it. In the eyes of God and the state of Nevada, you and I are legally married. A video of the ceremony should arrive at the front desk any minute." He gave her a lopsided grin. "Seems we were so eager to start the honeymoon, we forgot to take it with us."

Kristen's ears began to roar and her headache pounded unmercifully, repeating the same message over and over. *Married to Chance Warren...married to Chance... married—*

As she stared at him, her vision closed in from the sides and she suddenly couldn't draw a breath. She saw Chance start toward her, heard him call her name. But his voice sounded like an echo from a great distance. And when the tunnel closed in around her, the fog of unconsciousness became an escape too appealing for her to resist.

Chance watched Kristen's cheeks color a deep rose, while the rest of her face bleached pure white. She swayed once, then wilted.

"Kristen!" Alarmed, he stepped forward and caught her at the same moment her knees gave way.

"Aw, hell," he muttered, swinging her up into his arms. He hadn't expected her to be any happier about the turn of events than he was. But he hadn't figured she'd find the circumstances so appalling that she'd faint dead away.

He carried her to the bed, trying not to notice the enticing amount of breast visible through the parting in her robe or the feel of her soft body pressed to his chest. Married or not, they were still no more than social acquaintances. He could pretty much guess how she'd react if she came to and found him ogling her like a teenager looking at his first girlie magazine.

When he placed her on the bed, her robe gaped open even further, and not one, but two perfect breasts were exposed to his appreciative gaze. The air in his lungs rushed out in one big whoosh and his body tightened.

Chance closed his eyes and gallantly tried to concentrate on the unappealing task of digging a ditch—hard, back-breaking work that would exhaust a man and effectively wipe away all erotic thoughts.

It didn't help.

He had a sneaking suspicion he could shovel a crater the size of the Grand Canyon and still not erase the memory of Kristen's satiny, smooth skin against his palms, the feel of the dark coral tips begging for his attention.

Breathe in. Breathe out.

He had to regain control of his traitorous body. Several very important decisions had to be made. And damned quick. He didn't want, or need, the added complication of Kristen waking up to find him in an undeniable state of arousal. That sure as shootin' wouldn't help speed their conversation along.

Chance took another deep breath, opened his eyes and, with shaky hands, reached out to grasp the terry-cloth lapels and pull the robe together. He ground his teeth when his fingers brushed the silky slopes of her breasts. Turning, he rushed into the bathroom.

The cold water he splashed over his face brought back some of his sanity, and with it, a heavy dose of reality. He'd spent the night making love to his wife, and he'd lay money on the probability they hadn't bothered using protection.

Stunned, he raised his gaze to stare at himself in the mirror. "Good Lord, what if she's pregnant?"

Two

Chance leaned back to glance around the bathroom door at the unconscious woman—his wife—lying on the bed. Had pregnancy been the reason Kristen fainted? Would a side effect like this show up that fast?

Hell, how would I know? He tried to concentrate, but his head still throbbed from the champagne and he didn't have any hands-on experience with this type of thing, anyway.

His sister, Beth, had passed out once while she was pregnant with her daughter, Annie. But he'd been out on the rodeo circuit with his stock company and only heard about the incident later. The only other pregnant females he'd ever been around were of the four-legged variety. He'd never seen or heard of a cow or mare passing out during gestation.

Reaching for a washcloth, he shook his head. Gently. He had no idea if pregnancy could be the reason for

Kristen's fainting, but he for damned sure intended to find out.

He dampened the cloth with cool water, then headed straight for the phone beside the bed. Shrugging out of his jacket, he sat down on the bed beside Kristen and dialed the front desk. He bathed her face with the cloth while he waited for the hotel operator to pick up.

What seemed like an eternity later, a woman answered.

"I need the address of the nearest hospital," he said, trying to be patient despite the desperation clawing at his insides.

"Is this an emergency, sir?" the woman asked, her voice efficient. "Do you need an ambulance?"

His gut instinct told him Kristen wouldn't appreciate the added attention being hauled out on a stretcher would bring to their situation. "No, that won't be necessary." He laid the cool, damp cloth on Kristen's forehead. "My wife fainted. As soon as she's feeling strong enough, I'll take her myself."

When the woman rattled off the street name of the closest emergency clinic, Chance jotted down the information on a pad of paper he found on top of the nightstand. Hanging up the phone, he frowned as he ran the cloth over Kristen's pale cheeks. He couldn't believe how easily the word *wife* had rolled off his tongue. Damned if it hadn't felt almost natural.

Kristen stirred and murmured his name.

Taking her hand in his, Chance marveled at how small and fragile it felt. "I'm right here."

She opened her eyes and blinked. "Oh, no. It wasn't a dream."

He tried his best to give her an encouraging smile. "Afraid not, sweetheart." He brushed an auburn strand of hair from her damp cheek. "When you're feeling stronger, I'll take you to see a doctor."

She closed her eyes. "I don't need a doctor."

"Yes, you do," he said firmly. He wasn't quite sure how to phrase his next question, so he took a deep breath, thanked God she wasn't looking at him and asked straight out. "Are you on any kind of birth control?"

Her eyes snapped open. "That's none of your business."

When she tried to sit up, he put his hand on her shoulder to keep her from rising. "Yes, it is." He tried to be as tactful as possible, but some things couldn't be sugarcoated. "We just spent an entire night making love, Kristen. If you aren't on some type of preventive, there's a very real possibility that you might be pregnant."

She sucked in a sharp breath and her eyes widened. "Maybe nothing happened," she said, hope filling her expressive green gaze.

Chance swallowed hard. Although the memories he had of last night weren't clear by a long shot, and he had several blank spots about exactly what *had* taken place, his body told him he knew this woman in every sense of the word.

"Trust me, sweetheart," he said, unable to keep the knowing grin from his face. "It happened, all right. And more than once or twice."

Her cheeks colored a pretty pink. Amazing. He hadn't seen a woman blush in years.

"No, I'm not taking anything for birth control." He watched her fidget with the robe's belt, her attention devoted to rolling the end around her index finger.

Was it possible the ice maiden was embarrassed?

She continued to focus on the terry-cloth belt. "There hasn't been a reason."

"So you haven't been seeing anyone?"

Abandoning the belt, she glared up at him. "Why don't you ask what you really want to know? Have I been sleeping with anyone?"

Chance gave her a short nod.

She looked as if she wanted to sock him one. "The answer is no."

He refused to dwell on how relieved her admission made him feel. "Then if you are pregnant, the baby will be mine." Placing the cloth on the bedside table, he took a deep breath. "Well, I think the best thing we can do now is see a doctor, then go from there."

"I think it's too early to tell." She frowned, and he could tell she didn't have any experience in this particular area. The observation pleased the hell out of him.

"When—"

"I'm not sure about the time table, but I think it will take a few weeks for a test to show any accurate results."

"You fainted for a reason."

"I told you, I have a cold," she insisted. "Sometimes they settle in my inner ear."

"Are you on medication?"

She nodded. "My doctor gave me a prescription before I left Dallas to come to the finals."

Chance removed his hat, then ran his hand through his hair. "I'd like for you to check with a doctor before you take any more. Some of that stuff can hurt a baby."

Kristen felt her stomach do a back flip. The situation grew more complicated by the minute.

"Maybe there isn't anything to worry about." Refusing to stay put any longer, she sat up. "There's a big chance I'm not pregnant."

"But there's a possibility you *are*."

"Will you stop saying that?"

The man had the audacity to ignore her protest. "It's my child as much as yours, and I want what's best." She watched him replace his hat, then rest his forearms on his knees and stare down at his loosely clasped hands. "I'm not quite sure how to say this, so I'll just spit it out." He raised his gaze to meet hers. "I face up to my responsibilities. If you're pregnant, you won't have to go through this alone, Kristen. When the time comes, I'll be right there beside you, helping make decisions about raising the baby."

Decisions.

Kristen's head throbbed and she really didn't feel up to facing the possibilities he mentioned, let alone make decisions for a child that might not even exist.

"Okay, I'll see a doctor as soon as I return to Dallas." She might as well be reasonable about this. "When I find out something definite, I'll call you."

"No." He stood, placed his hands on his lean hips, then stared down at her. "Nothing against you or your honesty, but I don't know you well enough to know whether you'd contact me or not."

"Then what do you suggest?" No way was she taking him with her back to Dallas.

"After we see a doctor here in Vegas about your fainting spell, I want you to go with me to my ranch in the Panhandle," he said. "If it's too early for a definite answer now, we'll wait out the results there. Once we find out for sure what the verdict is, we'll deal with it."

She shook her head. "I can't do that."

"Why not?"

"I don't know you *that* well."

"We're married."

"Not for long."

"If you're pregnant—"

"I'm not."

"But if you are," he insisted, "I'd like for us to stay married until after the baby's born."

Trying to think, she rubbed her forehead. "I can't go with you. I'm expected back in Dallas tomorrow for a board meeting. I have to turn in my reports on the most likely candidates to endorse Sagebrush Boots."

"That can be taken care of by overnight express or a fax to your father."

Kristen felt the color drain from her face. What would Mike say if he knew his daughter had awakened this morning to find herself married to, and possibly pregnant by, the very man he'd warned her to avoid?

She glanced up at Chance. Her *husband*. The thought of being married to the sexiest cowboy she'd ever met set loose some very heated sensations in places that had no business being warm and tingly. She closed her eyes to keep the feelings from building. Getting all hot and bothered over the man she'd accidentally married was not solving the immediate problem.

To get her mind back on track, she thought of how Mike would take the news. Her father would undoubtedly take things a whole lot better if she'd married anyone but Chance Warren. The last name of Warren never failed to send Mike Lassiter into a tirade, but she'd never been able to figure out why.

Six years ago, when she'd first started soliciting endorsements for Sagebrush Boots, Mike had told her that under no circumstances was she to approach Chance. A successful, good-looking bull rider, he would have been the perfect spokesman for Sagebrush Boots and brought in a tremendous amount of business. But her father refused to budge on the issue. As long as Mike drew breath, a Warren would never get paid to endorse a pair of Sagebrush boots.

The gravity of what she'd done weighed her down and she closed her eyes. Mike would take one look at her and know something was up. And she'd already been a big-enough disappointment to the man just by being born female. If he found out she'd married Chance, she'd never see anything but contempt in his piercing gray gaze.

"Kristen, are you all right?" Chance asked, concern evident in his smooth baritone. "If going to my ranch bothers you that much, I'll go with you to Dallas."

Opening her eyes, she made a snap decision. She'd go with Chance to his ranch. At least until they sorted out what needed to be done about the annulment. Besides, it was much more appealing than the thought of trying to explain Chance's presence in her apartment to Mike.

"Now that I think about it, it might be best if I do accompany you to your ranch," she said coolly. She didn't want him to get the wrong idea. "I'll fax my report along with a message that I'm taking a little vacation time."

Chance nodded. "How long before you're ready, then?"

"Fifteen minutes or so. But—"

"I'll go down and take care of things at the front desk." Shrugging into his denim jacket, he bent down and picked up their marriage license. "I'll have a bellboy sent up to carry your luggage down to my truck," he said, tucking the document into his breast pocket. "Once we have you checked out at the hospital, I'd like to get on the road."

Before Kristen could protest his determination that she

see a doctor, he walked to the door and left without a backward glance.

Chance sat next to Kristen in the waiting room of the urgent-care clinic, his gaze fixed on the poster tacked to the wall opposite him. He hated having to bring her here. The place was packed with sick people. The man seated next to Kristen coughed, and Chance cringed. He'd always heard the best place in the world to be exposed to germs was in a hospital or doctor's office. What if she picked up something that made her miscarry?

He wasn't sure when he'd started hoping she was pregnant, but he had. Hell, he wasn't getting any younger. At thirty-four a man needed to start thinking about settling down and having a few kids.

Chance glanced at his wife. She wasn't his type of woman. He'd always pictured himself with a country gal—a woman who at least knew the difference between a bull and a steer. A woman he could rely on.

But fate had stepped in and matched him up with the exact opposite of what he'd always thought he wanted. Fate had paired him up with a city gal. He frowned. A woman with the same type of background as his own mother's.

He cut Kristen a sideways glance. One thing about it, though. She might not be his choice for the job, but they sure would make pretty babies together. The thought of how they'd get those babies made the region below his belt stir. It was a shame they wouldn't stay married to make more than the one they'd probably conceived last night.

When the man next to Kristen coughed again, Chance planted his hands on the arms of the chair and levered himself to his feet. "Trade places with me, Kristen."

"Why?"

He might have known she'd be stubborn about it. "Just do it, okay?"

"Chance, I'm perfectly fine right where I am."

He purposely narrowed his eyes and hoped his face showed more determination than worry. "If you haven't moved by the time I count to three, I'll pick you up and move you myself."

She glared back at him. "You wouldn't dare."

"Watch me, sweetheart." The guy next to her coughed for the third time. "One, two—"

"Oh, for heaven's sake!" Giving him a look that might have wilted a lesser man, she rose from her chair to sit in the one Chance had just vacated. "Now are you satisfied?"

He grinned. "Yep."

Relieved that she'd finally done as he asked, Chance seated himself between her and the man he was sure had something horribly contagious. Somewhere from behind them a small child sneezed, and Chance searched for a pair of empty chairs on the far side of the room. Every seat was taken.

Logically, he knew pregnant women faced this type of situation all the time. But Kristen wasn't just any woman. She was his wife. Possibly pregnant with his baby. That made it personal. Real personal.

He wasn't exactly comfortable with how much emotional investment he'd made in such a short time, but he wasn't going to deny it, either. At least, not to himself. He might not have wanted a wife, but he'd always wanted to be a father.

A woman in a brightly colored smock stepped through the door at the back of the waiting area. "Kristen Lassiter."

"It's about damned time," Chance muttered, bolting from the chair and pulling Kristen up with him.

When she swayed and leaned heavily against him, Chance glanced down to find that her face had bleached white as tissue paper. It was the same look she'd had back in the hotel just before she passed out. Without thinking twice, he scooped her up into his arms and headed toward the nurse.

"Second room on the right," the woman said, hurrying to keep up with him.

Chance gently placed Kristen on the examining table in the room the woman indicated. Staring down at her, he noticed her pale cheeks were gaining more color, but her eyes remained closed. "Kristen, sweetheart, are you all right?"

"Go away," she said through clenched teeth.

Her terse command made him feel a little better. At least she hadn't lost her spunk.

The woman in the floral smock closed the door, then went over to sit at the desk on the far side of the room. Flipping open a metal chart, she asked, "What seems to be the problem, Ms. Lassiter?"

"Her last name's Warren," Chance told the nurse.

"But she registered under the name of Lassiter," the woman said, frowning.

Chance looked at the name tag attached to the woman's ample bosom. "We got married last night, Mary-Ann," he said, using her first name and giving her a smile. "I guess it just takes a while for a woman to get used to her new last name."

His friendly approach worked. Accepting his explanation, Mary-Ann smiled back. "Oh, yes. It took me months before I started thinking of myself by anything other than my maiden name." She scribbled something on the chart, then came over to take Kristen's blood pressure and pulse. "What seems to be the problem, Mrs. Warren?"

Kristen finally opened her eyes. "I have a sinus infection and—"

"She keeps fainting," Chance explained, finishing for her. "She might be pregnant."

If looks could kill, Chance figured he'd be a dead man in three seconds flat. The sparks flashing in Kristen's eyes left no doubt how furious she was with him.

"Okay, I'll make a note of that," Mary-Ann said, taking Kristen's temperature. The nurse wrote in the chart, then turned toward the door. "The doctor will be in shortly."

The hushed click of the door closing behind the nurse seemed to revive Kristen. "Get out," she ordered, sitting up and pointing to the now-closed door.

Chance stood his ground. "No."

She made a kind of growling sound in the back of her throat that sounded as if she might just tear his head off and show it to him. "You have to be the most exasperating man on the face of the earth. Why did you tell that woman I might be pregnant?"

"It's the truth," he said reasonably. "And you wouldn't have said anything about it."

"Yes, I would." She glared at him. "But you make it sound like a certainty. How many times do I have to tell you, the possibility is so remote, it's not really worth considering?"

Before he could argue the point further, the door swung open and a tall gray-haired gentleman in a white lab coat walked into the room. He shook hands with Chance, then Kristen. "I'm Dr. Brayfield. I hear you aren't feeling well, Mrs. Warren. What seems to be the problem?"

"Before I left Dallas, I was diagnosed with a sinus infection," Kristen said, her gaze warning Chance to keep quiet. "I've been taking medication for it."

"I see here you might be pregnant," the doctor said, glancing at the metal chart he'd retrieved from the pocket on the door. "We'll do a pregnancy test—"

"No," Kristen said. "It won't be necessary."

"Yes, it is," Chance said at the same time.

Dr. Brayfield glanced up over the top of his half glasses, his look questioning.

"We got married last night," Chance explained. One look at Kristen told him he'd better sugarcoat the facts or he'd be in even bigger trouble than he already was. "We may want to start a family right away and I thought it best to make sure the medication is safe before she takes any more of it." There, that should satisfy both her and the doctor.

Smiling, Dr. Brayfield nodded. "I understand. If last night was the first relations you've had without using any type of preventive, there's no need to do a pregnancy test. The results wouldn't be as accurate as they will be in a week or two." He wrote something in the chart. "Now, what did your physician prescribe for your sinus infection, Mrs. Warren?"

Kristen gave Chance a warning look he was sure was meant to silence him, then told the doctor the name of the medication and her symptoms. "I've had this problem before," she added. "Sometimes the infection settles in my inner ear and causes dizziness."

"Is this the first time you've taken this prescription?" When she nodded, the doctor continued, "How long have you been on it?"

"Today will be the fourth day." She looked thoughtful for a moment, then asked, "Would drinking wine with this cause any kind of side effects?"

The doctor nodded. "Drinking any kind of alcohol with medication can cause side effects. Some serious, some less so. With this particular prescription there's a possibility of memory lapses and uncharacteristic behavior." He turned to Chance. "Have you noticed her acting differently than usual?"

Before Chance could answer, Kristen spoke up. "Yes. I married him last night. That was completely out of character for me."

Apparently the doctor thought Kristen was joking because he chuckled and took an instrument from the wall. He shone the tiny light into her ears, then looked at her throat. "Mmm." He jotted a note on the chart, then handed her some sample bottles of capsules. "I'm going to change the medication you're on. This should clear up both the sinus and inner ear problems within a few days."

"Is this safe in case she's pregnant?" Chance asked pointedly.

Dr. Brayfield nodded. "This is much safer and has fewer side effects." His grin wide, he winked. "No more accidental marriages."

"I'm glad I insisted on your seeing a doctor," Chance said, pulling his truck from the clinic parking lot. "You might have passed out when I wasn't around and hurt yourself or the baby."

Kristen glared at him. "Will you stop talking as if it's a fait accompli? All we know for sure is that I have an ear infection. We don't know if I'm pregnant."

"We don't know that you aren't, sweetheart," he said, shrugging. He grinned, and his face went from handsome to drop-dead gorgeous. "If passion and desire have anything to do with it, I'd say we have a bun in the oven for sure."

She supposed she should be upset that he insisted on calling her "sweetheart." But she wasn't going to ask him to stop. She couldn't explain it, but somehow when Chance used the endearment, it just felt...right.

Trying to turn her attention to something other than the man beside her, she focused on his "bun" comment. Most of her friends would have considered it crude, a remark best left to the lower social circles. But coming from Chance, it made her want to put on a baker's hat and...

Shaking her head to dislodge the erotic thought before it took hold, she remembered he hadn't listened to her objections over seeing a doctor. It appeared that Chance had a lot in common with Mike. He never listened to her, either.

Kristen stared out the truck window at the barren landscape of the Las Vegas outskirts. What would Mike do when he found out she'd married Chance? Would she be disowned?

The thought of his disapproval caused an instant sadness.

She—Mike's only child—had turned out to be a girl instead of the son he'd wanted. That had been the first time Kristen had disappointed him. Then, in the last twenty-seven years, she'd never seemed to measure up, never been able to do anything to win his acceptance and love.

Now, with the mess she'd gotten herself into last night, she feared she'd never see an expression of approval on Mike's face. Not for her, not for anything she accomplished. Unexpectedly, her breath caught on a soft sob.

"What's wrong, Kristen?"

His big hand covered hers where it rested in her lap. "Don't worry." He twined their fingers and gave her hand a gentle squeeze. "We'll get through this together. I'm here for you, sweetheart."

Kristen swallowed hard. Why did her insides turn to melted butter every time he spoke in that soft, sexy drawl?

"I guess I'm just a little tired," she lied. She wasn't about to try explaining something she didn't understand herself. "I'll be fine."

Chance turned her hand loose to reach down and release the catch on her seat belt. "Why don't you move over here to the middle of the seat and rest your head on my shoulder? You look like you could use some sleep."

"I can't do that."

"You aren't feeling well, Kristen." He stroked her cheek with the back of his hand. "We have a long way to go. Maybe if you take a nap you'll feel better."

It might have been his softly spoken words, or the feel of his hand on her cheek. She couldn't be sure. But she suddenly felt drained of all energy.

"Maybe for just a few minutes."

When she scooted over and secured the center seat belt, Chance put his arm around her. She placed her head against his shoulder and it pleased the hell out of him. It shouldn't have. But it did. "That's it, sweetheart. Just relax and try to rest."

Seconds after closing her eyes, her breathing became shallow, signaling that she'd fallen asleep.

Chance set the cruise control and adjusted the position of the steering wheel down to a more comfortable angle. He draped his left wrist over the top, then settled back for the long drive ahead. He had a lot to think about and several hundred miles to get it all sorted out.

Although Kristen hadn't exactly warmed up to him, he'd noticed a vulnerability about her in the hotel room once she'd regained consciousness. There had been an uncertainty in her demeanor that he never in a million years would have associated with the ice maiden. She'd turned pale as a ghost when he'd mentioned sending those reports to her father.

A bull of a man, Mike Lassiter wore his expensive western-cut suits with a style and grace that belied his considerable size. But that hadn't been what made a lasting impression on Chance. It had been the open hostility Lassiter displayed on the few occasions they'd been around each other. Chance couldn't remember ever having talked to the man. But for some reason, each time he caught Lassiter staring at him, the man's eyes had been filled with intense loathing.

Chance absently stroked Kristen's silky auburn hair with his right hand. From the look of fear she'd displayed at the thought of going back to Dallas to face her father, Chance figured the rumors about Lassiter had to be right on the money. Over the years, Chance had heard plenty about Mike Lassiter and his demands of perfection; how he made it impossible for anyone to ever live up to his expectations. It was even rumored the man's late wife had died from being so unhappy.

Chance glanced down at his own sleeping wife. How could any man intentionally create the apprehension in a woman that he'd seen in Kristen? And why?

His hand, draped over the steering wheel, tightened into a fist at the thought of anyone intimidating Kristen. He had a feeling he was about to jump buck-naked into a hornet's nest, but he'd be damned if he'd let Mike Lassiter run roughshod over Kristen. Even though their marriage was temporary, as her husband, Chance had an obligation to protect her. And if that meant crossing her own father to do it, then that's exactly what he'd do.

Three

——

"**K**risten, wake up."

Kristen slowly straightened to look out the windshield of the pickup truck. "Where are we?" she asked, wishing her dream hadn't been interrupted. She'd been securely wrapped in the strong arms of a tall, broadshouldered man, his deep Texas drawl whispering over her senses when he called her *sweetheart* as they made love.

"Gallup, New Mexico," Chance said, turning off the ignition. He cupped her cheek with his hand. "You fell asleep again right after we stopped for gas in Flagstaff, sweetheart."

Chance's touch, the sound of his voice when he called her "sweetheart," and the realization that she'd been dreaming about making love with him helped to clear her sleep-fogged brain. She had absolutely no business fantasizing about the man, even if it was in a dream and he was her temporary husband. They weren't going to be married any longer than it took for the ink to dry on the annulment papers.

After dreaming about being loved by the man, she realized sitting close to him wasn't going to bring her pulse back down to a normal rate or stop the awareness she felt in every nerve ending in her body. She scooted over to the passenger side of the bench seat.

Blinking against the bright flashing neon sign in front of her, it took a moment to comprehend where Chance had parked the truck. "Why are we stopped at a pharmacy?"

He unbuckled his seat belt and reached for the door handle. "I have a few things I want to pick up before we find a motel."

"Motel?" Her mind came to full alert. She thanked the moon and stars above that her voice didn't sound as panicked as she felt. Chance had to be the sexiest, best-looking and most charming cowboy she'd ever met. She had a feeling that's what got her into this mess to begin with. Spending another night with him would definitely not be in her best interest.

He pushed the door open with his shoulder. "You didn't think we'd drive straight through, did you?"

"Yes. No." Confused, she shook her head. "I hadn't thought much about it."

She'd been so preoccupied with how to avoid Mike, she hadn't even considered when, or if, they'd be stopping for the night. But with more than eight hundred miles between Las Vegas and Amarillo, it stood to reason they wouldn't be driving straight through to Chance's ranch.

Lost in thought, she missed what Chance asked next. "What?"

"Are you going inside or staying here?" His smile made her insides tingle.

"I'll wait here."

She needed time to think. If he was planning a repeat of last night, he'd better think again. They might be married, but they wouldn't be sleeping together.

"Need anything?" Chance asked, getting out of the truck.

"No." *And if you're buying what I think you're buying, you might as well save your money.*

"You're sure?" he asked one last time.

"Yes."

He shrugged. "Okay. I'll be right back."

He closed the driver's door, then walked to the entrance, his long-legged stride relaxed and confident. Like a man who knew what he wanted and how to go about getting it. The mere thought made her warm all over. And that was wrong. All wrong.

Narrowing her eyes, she watched him disappear inside the drugstore. "You'd better not be buying anything more than a toothbrush, cowboy."

Several minutes later, Chance strolled back across the parking lot to the truck as if he didn't have a care in the world. When he grinned at her through the truck window, her stomach fluttered. She pressed herself against the passenger side door. No man had the right to exude that much charm and sex appeal, or make her flutter in places no man had ever made her flutter before.

When he opened the door and slid into the driver's seat, he tossed a sack onto the dash. "Ready to find a room?"

"Two rooms," Kristen said, making sure to put all her determination into her tone. "And I'm paying for mine."

His mouth thinned to a flat line as he started the truck,

put it in reverse and backed from the parking lot. "No, you won't."

Kristen shook her head. "I mean it, Chance. I intend to pay—"

"Like hell you'll pay for a room," he said, his own voice just as determined. "We're married. I'll take care of the bill."

"Don't be silly," she said reasonably. "We won't be married for long, and besides, neither one of us intended for it to happen."

"Doesn't matter."

Chance was every bit as stubborn as Mike, she decided, her level of frustration rising another notch. She'd never been able to get Mike to budge on anything once he'd made up his mind, either.

Chance pulled into a motel parking area a few blocks from the pharmacy. "You're my responsibility as long as your last name is Warren."

Without another word he got out of the truck and slammed the door with a resounding thud.

His responsibility.

Her heart sinking, Kristen watched him enter the motel lobby. How many times in her life had Mike said the same thing almost word for word?

She squeezed her eyes shut. It shouldn't matter. Chance Warren wasn't much more than a stranger. But for some reason his viewing her as a responsibility made her want to cry. Why couldn't she ever be more to someone than an obligation?

When Chance returned a few minutes later and slid behind the steering wheel, Kristen couldn't help but notice his hesitant expression. "What's wrong?"

He started the truck and pulled around the side of the building. "These places along the interstate fill up fast."

"Really?" She had a sinking feeling at what he was about to tell her, but she asked, anyway. "Why do you say that?"

"You're never going to believe this," he said, parking in front of a bank of numbered doors.

"Tell me and we'll see if I will or not."

He removed the keys from the ignition, then turned to face her. "I'm really sorry, Kristen, but they had only one room available."

She shook her head. "You're right. I'm not buying it."

"Honest," he said, holding his right hand in the air as if he were taking an oath on a witness stand. "We wouldn't have been able to get this room if they hadn't had a late cancellation."

One look at the parking area told her he was telling the truth. The place was packed, and she was going to have to spend the night in the same room with her husband. The fluttering in her stomach went absolutely berserk.

"We could go somewhere else," she said, sounding desperate even to herself. "Surely this isn't the only—"

He shook his head. "The desk clerk called around. Every motel in town is filled up."

"Then we'll just keep driving," she said. Her heart rate increased and her palms began to sweat. "I'm sure there'll be something available farther down the road."

"Look, I understand how you feel," Chance said, his voice tight. "But we got a late start, we're both tired, and the possibility of finding something between here and Albuquerque is slim to none."

She looked miserable at the thought of spending the night with him. Why that bothered him, Chance wasn't sure. But it did.

He plucked the sack from the top of the dash, got out of the truck and came around to open the passenger door. "We'll just have to make the best of it."

"Please tell me there are two beds," she said, her voice not much more than a whisper.

She definitely wasn't going to like his answer to that one. He cleared his throat. "Uh...well, now that you mention it, I'm not real sure."

"You didn't ask?"

When he shook his head, her eyes turned to a sparkling, stormy green. It fascinated the hell out of him. She was mad as a wet hen, and absolutely gorgeous. He suddenly remembered just how beautiful when the image of her nude body lying next to his flashed through his mind.

The thought of spending another night in the same bed with her—his body pressed to her softness, his hands cupping the weight of her perfect breasts—had his hormones racing around like a steel bearing in a pinball machine headed for full tilt. Trying to ease the increasing tightness of his jeans, he shifted from one foot to the other.

He helped her from the truck and bit back a groan. The feel of her soft hand in his sent a jolt of electricity up his arm. It quickly spread down to explode in his lower gut. Maybe driving on to Albuquerque wouldn't be such a bad idea.

One look at the shadows beneath her eyes and he abandoned that notion immediately. She was exhausted. When she swayed, he put his arm around her waist and a tender, protective feeling surged through him.

"Steady there, sweetheart."

"Turn me loose."

She tried to pull away from him, but Chance held on to her as they walked to the motel room. He told himself he was just making sure she didn't pass out and fall, but he knew better. She just felt too damned good to turn loose.

He slipped the key into the lock, swung the door open and flipped on the light. The room had one window, one lamp, one table with one chair.

And *one* bed.

"This isn't going to work," Kristen said flatly.

She turned to leave, but Chance put his hands on her shoulders to stop her. Staring down into her eyes, he decided a man could get caught up and drown in the emerald depths.

"Kristen, we're both tired and you aren't feeling well. We can handle this." He tried to make sure his voice sounded convincing despite the serious reservations beginning to claw at his gut. "Nothing is going to happen."

She stared up at him for several long seconds before determination replaced the shadows of doubt in her steady gaze. "You're right. We can handle this situation. We're both adults."

Chance nodded. "You can have the bed. I'll take the floor." He wasn't looking forward to the stiff back he'd wake up with the next morning, but maybe a little discomfort would help him control an even bigger discomfort in other regions of his body.

"We'll make out just fine," she agreed, looking around the room.

The top of the paper sack crackled from his hand tightening into a death grip around it. Apparently, the double entendre hadn't occurred to her, but it wasn't lost on Chance. When he felt in danger of drawing her to him and showing her just how fine he'd like to make it, he backed toward the door.

"At least the room's clean," she offered.

"Which suitcase will you need for tonight?" he asked suddenly. It seemed they were both trying to ignore the obvious.

"The small carry-on has everything I'll need for now," she replied, walking across to the vanity area of the room.

The gentle sway of her hips and the length of her slender legs made sweat bead on his forehead. He swallowed hard. Although certain details were still hazy, he remembered that less than twenty-four hours ago those same hips had cradled him, her long legs wrapped around him as she held him tightly to her. He muttered a curse. He was within an ace of picking her up, carrying her to the bed and making love to her until they both collapsed from exhaustion.

"Did you say something?" she asked, without turning to face him.

"I'll…uh, just go out and get what you want, then see if I can rustle us up some sandwiches. I think I saw a burger joint about a block down from this place."

Good Lord! I've got to get out of here.

He needed to get away from her in order to regain control of the fire building in places he'd rather not dwell on. If he didn't, he figured he'd be setting off the smoke detector just about any minute.

"I'll be back," he said, tossing the pharmacy sack onto the table.

Chance closed the door, walked to his truck and leaned heavily against the side. How was he going to spend the night with Kristen and keep his hands to himself? Just the thought of sleeping in the same room with her had him hard as hell and throbbing with anticipation. He couldn't recall a lot of what happened last night, but he did remember it had been the sweetest, most passionate loving he'd ever experienced.

He gritted his teeth against the fresh wave of heat coursing through him, jerked open the passenger door and reached into the back of the extended cab for the suitcase she'd requested. He wasn't sure what a man was supposed to do with a woman who wasn't going to be his wife for longer than it took to have their marriage annulled, but he knew for certain a roll in the hay wasn't it.

When he returned to the motel, he deposited the carry-on bag just inside the motel room and told Kristen he was going to get them dinner.

Kristen watched Chance pull the door shut behind him. She was dying of curiosity, but she forced herself to wait until she heard his truck engine start before she grabbed the sack he'd tossed on the table. She had to find out why he'd stopped at the pharmacy.

With shaking fingers, she unfolded the top, then reached inside. The items she pulled from the bag stopped her cold. Chance hadn't purchased condoms as she expected. She almost wished he had. It certainly would have made it easier to resist him if she'd found he was blatantly planning a repeat of the night before. But he wasn't. He'd bought several books on pregnancy and prenatal care. She scanned the titles on the covers, and a couple of them shook her to the very foundation of her soul—*A Father's Guide from Conception to Birth* and *How to Ease Your Wife's Labor and Delivery*.

Placing the books back inside the sack, she sank into the chair beside the table. Just when she thought she had the man figured out, he went and did something like this. Never in a million years would she have guessed he'd take the possibility of fatherhood so seriously. It was almost as if he actually wanted her to be pregnant.

She shook her head, rose from the chair and crossed the room to stand in front of the full-length mirror on the back of the bathroom door. She didn't look pregnant. Turning sideways, she pulled her blouse from her tailored slacks and flattened the blue silk to her stomach. How would she look if she were expecting?

No, that wasn't going to work, she decided. Her stomach was way too flat. Walking over to the bed, she grabbed a pillow, stuffed it under her blouse, then waddled back to stand in front of the mirror. She turned from side to side, assessing the bulge beneath her breasts. What would it feel like to have Chance's baby moving inside her?

A contented feeling began to warm the farthest corners of her soul. If she were pregnant—which she wasn't—it would be the first time since her mother's passing that she'd have someone to love and who loved her unconditionally in return.

So intent on the image of herself in the mirror and her thoughts of impending motherhood, it took Kristen a moment to realize she wasn't alone. When she looked up, Chance stood right behind her, his eyes filled with a heat that took her breath away. Her heart pounded hard in her chest and her cheeks burned.

"I didn't—" she jerked the pillow from beneath her blouse and sailed it toward the bed "—hear you come in."

"I hope a hamburger and fries will be all right. They didn't have a lot to choose from." The passionate gleam in his eyes didn't waver, but his words were as innocuous as hers.

Good. It appeared they were both going to ignore the humiliating situation.

"That's fine. I think I'll take a shower first, then eat." She felt his gaze follow her across the room to where he'd set the overnight case. Gathering the few items she'd need, Kristen forced herself to walk calmly toward the bathroom when what she really wanted to do was find a hole, crawl into it and pull the opening in behind her. "But you go ahead before it gets cold."

She closed the door, then leaned against it for support. The last thing she wanted to do was give Chance the impression she thought he might be right about her being pregnant. She'd just been curious, that's all.

Chance watched Kristen take another bite of a french fry and thought he might explode right then and there. Her teeth nipped at the end of the crisp potato strip a moment before her tongue licked away the lingering traces of salt from her lips.

He mentally ran through every curse word he knew as he crossed the room, closed the bathroom door behind him, stripped off his clothes and reached into the shower to turn on the water. He wasn't looking forward to stepping beneath the icy spray. It was going to chill him to the bone, make his teeth chatter and send certain parts of his anatomy into traumatic shock.

A phrase from his rodeo days came to mind as he anticipated how the water would feel. Whenever a rider drew a rank horse or bull, or suffered from the aches and pains that went along with riding the rough stock, he gritted his teeth, swallowed the pain and uttered two simple little words before doing what had to be done. Chance glanced down at the lower part of his body and the phrase "Cowboy up" took on a whole new meaning.

Cursing a blue streak, he stepped into the shower. He yelped when the cold spray hit his skin, raising goose bumps. He shivered uncontrollably. The chill coursing through his body helped to restore some of his sanity and reduce the fever burning in his belly, but not nearly as much as he'd hoped.

Before tonight, he'd never in his life been aroused by the sight of a pregnant woman. And he'd probably have slugged the first person who even dared to suggest that he would be.

But Kristen standing in front of the mirror with the pillow stuffed under her shirt, her slender fingers splayed along the sides of her pretend belly, had excited the hell out of him. She'd looked so beautiful, so feminine, so...pregnant—with his child.

He shook his head, shut off the water and grabbed a towel. He supposed any woman would wonder what she'd look like in the advanced stages of pregnancy. But until tonight the thought had never crossed *his* mind.

Now it was all he could think about. How would Kristen look six months from now if she did have his baby nestled safely inside of her? How would the taut skin of her belly feel under his hands? As her pregnancy advanced, would they have to be creative with their positions when he made love to her?

Like thinking about that helps my condition any!

With a raw curse he tossed the towel aside, turned on the water and stepped back beneath the ice-cold spray. The water coursed over him and he shuddered violently. The thought of Kristen's slender body growing round with his child had him hard as hell and throbbing with an intensity that threatened to make his knees buckle.

If this kept up, one of two things would have to happen. He'd either come down with a case of double pneumonia from all the cold showers he'd be taking, or he'd have to give serious thought to seeing a therapist.

Ten minutes later, he stepped out of the bathroom to find Kristen nestled snugly in bed, her beautiful face relaxed in peaceful sleep. She was curled on her side, one delicate hand beneath her flawless cheek. He swallowed hard against the compelling desire to pull the covers back and slide in beside her. Her long auburn hair, spilling over her creamy shoulder, reminded him of waking up just this morning to find those waves spread across his chest.

Chance gritted his teeth and made a beeline for his duffel bag by the chair in the corner. Removing a clean change of clothes, he ripped the towel from around his waist, yanked on his jeans and shirt, then stuffed his bare feet into his boots. With one last look at his wife lying on the bed, he jerked open the door and stepped out into the crisp New Mexico night.

Maybe if he walked a couple of miles in the near-freezing temperature, his mind would clear and he'd stop acting like a hormone-crazed teenager lusting after the prom queen.

Stuffing his hands into the front pockets of his jeans, his fingertips pressed against the smooth, warm surface of the agate, reminding him that luck was on his side. The lucky piece had never let him down before, why would it start now?

True, he hadn't envisioned himself with a city gal like Kristen. Hell, he couldn't find one thing they had in common. Except for the fact that they'd awakened this morning—married—and had most likely made a baby together sometime during the night.

Suddenly, the thought of staying married to Kristen wasn't such an unpleasant idea. After all, fate had brought them together, and the only reason he could see for that happening was to make a baby. He turned the idea over in his mind. He'd never been one to turn down an opportunity when fate handed it to him. No, sir.

Maybe they should stay married. A man could do a lot worse for the mother of his child, and the way he saw it, they'd be married for nine more months if she was pregnant. The least they could do would be to give the whole thing a damned good shot for the baby's sake. Unlike his own mother, he was determined to be a good parent and be there for his kids. As long as he lived, he'd never forget how it felt when he'd awakened one morning to find his mother gone. He'd been twelve at the time and it had taken him years to get over the hurt and rejection.

He rounded the corner of the motel and skidded to a halt just in time to keep from running into a man and woman entering one of the rooms. The man held one of those car seat-baby carriers Chance had seen his sister use with her babies.

When the man nodded a greeting, Chance touched two fingers to the brim of his Resistol in answer and kept going. If he and Kristen stayed together, this time next year that could be their little family checking into a room on the way home from the PBR Finals. The thought quickly had a warmth spreading from his chest throughout his body.

As the feeling began to build, Chance turned and retraced his steps back to the motel room where his wife slept. If seeing that family and the feeling of longing it had created in him wasn't a sure sign that fate meant for him and Kristen to stay together to raise their child, he didn't know what did.

* * *

"No-o-o-o," Kristen cried, waking herself from the nightmare. Her heart pounded heavily in her chest and her silk nightshirt clung to her perspiration-dampened body.

Strong arms suddenly closed around her and lifted her to a wide, bare chest. "Kristen, it's just a dream. You're safe, sweetheart," Chance crooned. He brushed the hair from her cheek and placed a soft kiss to her temple. "Nothing's going to hurt you. I promise."

Her pulse began to slow, but Mike's harsh words echoed through her mind, causing emotional pain so deep, she shuddered. In her dream, Mike had disowned her and sworn he never wanted to see or hear from her again.

Realizing that the man holding her had been the cause of Mike's wrath, she squeezed her eyes shut and tried to gather the fragments of her composure. "Please, let me go." She took a deep breath. "It was just a silly dream. I'm okay."

"Are you sure?" Chance asked, still holding her securely to him. "You're shaking like a leaf caught up in a dust devil."

Kristen took a deep, steadying breath and nodded. "I'll be fine."

He loosened his hold but didn't move away. He gently tucked a strand of hair behind her ear, his palm caressing the side of her neck. "Want to talk about it?"

His tender touch, the genuine concern she heard in his voice, chased away the lingering chill in her soul and warmed her in places that had no business heating up. She opened her eyes and her breath lodged in her throat. Chance was wearing nothing but a pair of white cotton briefs.

Lifting her gaze to meet his, she watched his concern turn to an awareness that mirrored her own. She heard his breath catch, felt his biceps tighten beneath her fingers a moment before his head began to lower.

She told herself she should stop him, that kissing a man who sat on her bed wearing nothing but underwear wasn't in her best interest. But the thought evaporated immediately when his warm, firm lips covered hers and he settled her against him. Her nipples tightened to an almost painful state at the feel of rock-hard pectoral muscles flexing against them through her silk gown.

He nibbled at the seam of her mouth, coaxing her to open for him. Without a second thought, she responded to his unspoken request, and his tongue slipped inside to mate with her own. Teasing, coaxing, exploring, Chance kissed her with a thoroughness that sent liquid fire racing from every part of her body to gather in the pit of her stomach.

His hands moved from her back to lift her arms to his shoulders, giving him free access to her breasts. When he covered them, Kristen moaned and arched into his callused palms.

Somewhere outside a car door slammed, then an engine revved, bringing her to her senses. What in the world did she think she was doing, anyway? One minute she'd been trembling from the remnants of the nightmare, and the next she'd been shivering with desire for the man offering her comfort.

When she attempted to pull away, Chance slid his hands from her breasts around to her back. Soothing, once again, he smoothed his palms down her spine. "Feeling a little better, sweetheart?"

Afraid her voice would betray just how much he affected her, she nodded.

"It's getting close to dawn. I'll go see about rustling up some coffee and doughnuts for breakfast." He pressed a kiss to her forehead, then set her away from him and stood. "Do you think you can be packed and ready to leave as soon as I get back?"

Standing beside the bed the way he was, she was on eye level with his white cotton briefs. The bulge of his arousal strained the fabric impressively. Kristen's eyes widened and her response lodged somewhere between her vocal cords and opened mouth.

She quickly raised her eyes, but when her gaze clashed with his, her breath caught. His confident smile spoke volumes and made her cheeks burn.

"No need for you to be embarrassed," he said, shrugging into his shirt. "We're married. It's perfectly normal and acceptable for a husband to desire his wife."

She gulped. He was acting as if he intended for them to stay married. "But we'll be getting an annulment as soon as possible."

He shook his head. "I did a lot of thinking last night." Pulling on his jeans, he gingerly slid the zipper up. "For whatever reason, fate dealt us a hand that neither one of us anticipated. But that doesn't mean it's not a winner." He tugged on his socks and boots, then grabbed his truck keys. "I've always been a man who followed his instincts, and mine are telling me this is right on the money." Opening the door, he flashed her a devastating smile. "You just need to get used to the idea—like I had to—that I'm the man who'll be making love to you every night and helping you raise our babies."

Kristen felt her jaw drop. "But—"

He crossed the room to give her a quick, hard kiss, then grabbed his hat and walked back to the door. "Don't worry, sweetheart. It'll be my pleasure—and yours—to convince you this is the way things were meant to be."

Before she managed to find her voice, he stepped out into the predawn darkness, leaving her to wonder if insanity had been one of Mike's reasons for wanting her to steer clear of Chance Warren.

Four

———

"**W**here does that go?" Kristen asked, pointing to a little side road with deeply cut ruts. After leaving the outskirts of Amarillo, they'd traveled south along a blacktop highway that seemed to lead them out into the middle of nowhere.

"It dead-ends about two miles down, at an old barn," Chance answered without turning his head. "It's part of my sister and brother-in-law's spread. We'll have a Halloween dance there this weekend."

"I didn't know you had a sister."

"There's a lot about me you don't know," he said, flashing her a grin.

She tried to ignore the warm, fuzzy feeling his easy smile caused. "That street goes both ways."

"Yeah, I guess it does." He winked. "But just think about how much fun we'll have meeting in the middle."

Kristen's toes curled at the thought. And that wasn't

a good sign. Since his outlandish announcement this morning that he thought they should stay married, Chance hadn't just turned on the charm, he'd opened the floodgate. He'd seized every opportunity possible to remind her of the kiss they'd shared in the motel room, and to talk about their future together.

She'd tried telling him—in a nice way—that he'd lost his mind. But the man refused to listen.

He steered the pickup off the main road, across a cattle guard and beneath an arched, wrought-iron sign proclaiming the property to be the Sundance Ranch and Rodeo Company. As he guided the truck around a pothole large enough to drive into and not be heard from for days, she risked glancing at him. He looked like a man who was in complete control of his life. Hers, on the other hand, had been thrown into utter chaos.

When one of the front tires dropped off into another hole, he laughed. "Home sweet home."

Kristen felt a twinge of envy run through her when she noticed his obvious pleasure at being back on his ranch. What would it be like to have a home she was happy to return to?

Her condo in Dallas held about as much appeal as the reception area of a dentist's office. Technically, it wasn't even hers. It belonged to Sagebrush Boots.

When she'd graduated from college, Mike had insisted on buying the penthouse. At the time, he'd told her it was her graduation present. But he'd picked out the decorator, the color scheme and the style of furnishings. She'd had no say in any of the decisions. After she'd moved in, she'd discovered why. Mike felt it would be the perfect setting for dinner meetings with clients. On a moment's notice, Kristen was expected to open her home, play hostess and keep quiet while business was discussed. Her home wasn't a home at all. It was just another big tax break for Sagebrush Boots.

They drove in silence for several minutes before Chance stopped the truck and killed the motor at the top of a hill overlooking a wide valley. Pointing to a ranch complex nestled on the far side, he said, "Welcome to the Sundance."

"How long have you owned this?" she asked, amazed by the size of the spread. Even in the approaching shadows of dusk, Kristen could tell it was huge.

"Five years." He stared out at the well-kept pastures, barns and big two-story house. "After I had to quit riding the rough stock, I bought the land. Then a year later I had the chance to buy some bulls, horses and roping calves from a local contractor." He shrugged. "Before I knew it, the Sundance Rodeo Company was born, and I'd become a stock contractor."

Despite his casual attitude toward his accomplishments, Kristen couldn't miss the pride in his voice. Her envy increased. She'd love to have something she'd worked hard to build, a dream she'd turned into reality. When she'd earned her degree in business, she'd had high hopes of putting her ideas to work at Sagebrush Boots. But Mike would never consider her having more than a token position with the company. And that had only been a grudging concession when she'd talked of finding a job elsewhere.

"How many employees do you have?" she asked.

"Four wranglers who travel the circuit with me and two ranch hands." He started the engine and eased the powerful truck around another pothole only slightly smaller than the others. "And then there's Sarah."

"Is she your housekeeper?"

The look he gave her bordered on panic. "Whatever

you do, don't call her that where she can hear you. She'll pitch a fit and be on the warpath for days.''

Kristen laughed at his desperate expression. ''Why?''

''When me and the boys are on the road, Sarah runs the place.'' He chuckled. ''Hell, she pretty much runs the place when I'm here.''

''You mean she's your ranch foreman?'' Kristen asked, amazed. Mike would never hear of a woman holding any type of position he considered better left to a man.

''I guess you could call her that. She keeps the house clean, cooks meals, and when I'm not around, she keeps the ranch hands in line and sees that the chores get done.''

''Isn't that an unusual position for a woman?''

Chance laughed out loud. ''If you knew Sarah Carpenter you wouldn't be asking that. She can ride and rope better than half of the cowboys in the Panhandle. And when it comes to creative phrases, she can out-cuss a fleet of sailors on a three-day drunk.''

''The woman sounds quite…colorful,'' Kristen said, grinning.

He nodded. ''She's got eight acres of hell in her when she's riled, but she's got a heart of pure gold. When my dad was killed a few years after my mom took off, Sarah moved in and took care of my sister and me until we'd both finished high school.''

Kristen marveled at the respect she detected in his voice. She wasn't used to hearing a man express that kind of attitude toward a woman.

Chance had just pulled the truck to a stop at the side of the house when the back door swung open and a woman Kristen would judge to be in her early fifties stepped out onto the porch. Dressed in jeans and a red plaid flannel shirt, her salt-and-pepper hair drawn up into a tight bun, Sarah Carpenter stood with her booted feet spread wide, fists planted on ample hips. In one hand she gripped a large wooden spoon. She looked like a cross between Aunt Bea and Calamity Jane.

"It's about time you dragged your sorry carcass home, boy," Sarah called, shaking the spoon at Chance. Kristen was amazed that they had no trouble hearing her through the closed truck windows. "Zach and the boys pulled in with the semi around two this mornin'. They said you'd stayed behind to take care of some business, but didn't seem to know what it was. What've you been up to now?"

"You let her get away with talking to you that way?" Kristen asked. Mike would have had the woman fired on the spot.

"She gets kind of touchy when she's worried about one of us." He winced. "She's going to take a strip off my hide for not calling and letting her know why I didn't come in with the rest of the men."

Amazed by his reluctance to face the woman, Kristen watched him take a deep breath, then shoulder open the truck door. "Now, Sarah, don't get all riled up. I can explain."

"It'd better be good," the woman said, her face set in implacable lines.

"It is." Chance walked around, opened the passenger door and helped Kristen from the truck. "I've got someone I want you to meet."

The tingles where their hands touched made her jerk free of his grasp. She rubbed her palm against her denim skirt to ease the sensation.

"Sarah, I'd like for you to meet my wife."

"Stop saying that," Kristen said through gritted teeth. "We aren't going—"

"Hush, sweetheart." Chance gave her a quick kiss to insure her silence.

It worked. The feel of his lips on hers, even briefly, made her forget whatever protest she might have made.

Obviously struck speechless, Sarah opened her mouth, then snapped it shut. When she finally found her voice, there was a strained quality to it, as if it were on the verge of cracking, and her brown eyes looked suspiciously moist. "Chance Warren, I ought to skin you alive. I've been waitin' for years to dance at·your weddin', and here you up and get hitched without sayin' a word."

She rushed forward, wrapped her arms around Kristen, then, holding her at arm's length, Sarah asked, "What's your name, honey?"

"Kristen Lassiter."

"Warren," Chance cut in. He wouldn't even mind if Kristen wanted to hyphenate their last names the way so many women were doing these days. But it was important to him that she use his surname.

A shadow of emotion flashed in Sarah's brown gaze and there was a slight wavering of her smile, but Chance had to give her credit, she covered it nicely. To anyone else, Sarah's expression probably looked perfectly normal, but Chance knew her too well. Unless he missed his guess, he'd hear all about what was eating her just as soon as she got him alone.

"It's nice to meet you, Sarah," Kristen said, swaying slightly. Chance slipped his arm around her waist to steady her.

"What's wrong, child?" Sarah asked, her eagle-sharp eyes catching the movement. "You feelin' bad?"

Kristen tried to lean away, but Chance held her firmly against him. She gave him a warning look—which he promptly ignored—before turning her attention to Sarah. "I'm fine, really. I have a slight inner ear infection that makes me dizzy sometimes."

Sarah glared at Chance, but before she got wound up in one of her famous lectures, he nodded. "I made sure she saw a doctor before we left Vegas."

"You missed supper. Did you stop somewhere along the way to feed her?"

"Yes, ma'am."

"Well, don't just stand there." Sarah stepped between him and Kristen, put her arm around Kristen's shoulders, then waved the spoon at him. "You bring the suitcases in while I take this girl up to your room and put her to bed. She looks 'bout ready to drop."

Chance watched Sarah guide Kristen up the porch steps and through the back door. Sarah was going to take Kristen to *his* room. The thought of her lying in his bed, her silky hair spread across his pillow, the sheets caressing her delicate body, had the blood rushing through his veins faster than a quarter horse sprinting for the finish line.

Cursing a blue streak, he walked to the side of the truck and began pulling Kristen's luggage from the extended cab. He'd told himself that he wasn't going to push her, that he'd give her time to get used to the idea of their staying married. But the thought of her tucked snugly into his bed had him hard as hell and wishing he hadn't been so gallant.

His gaze traveled up the side of the house to the second story. There were four bedrooms up there besides his, but there wasn't one of them that held near the appeal his own held at the moment. Why hadn't he thought to tell Sarah to put Kristen in one of them?

He stopped suddenly, the air whooshing from his lungs. Of course Sarah would put *his* wife to bed in *his* room. She had no idea of the circumstances surrounding their nuptials, or that he was having to give the bride time to warm up to the idea of being married to him. And from what little he knew about Kristen, he figured she'd leave it up to him to explain things.

He'd have to let Sarah know that the marriage wasn't a commitment of undying love, but more of an accident he and Kristen had no choice but to deal with. He knew that wasn't going to set well with the older woman. Well, hell. At first, it hadn't set all that well with him or Kristen, either.

A niggling little thought that she might not hang around tried to implant itself in his mind. He ignored it. The way he saw it, they had to play out the hand fate had dealt them.

He'd come to terms with it. Kristen would, too.

After waking up two mornings in a row to wrap his arms around Kristen's soft, feminine body, sleeping alone wasn't something he looked forward to. Resigned, Chance hefted the suitcases and headed for the house. He'd just have to take one of the other bedrooms and hope exhaustion allowed him to sleep at night. At least, until Kristen came around and let him back in his bed.

Half an hour later, Chance had deposited the luggage upstairs, checked on his sleeping wife, then moved a few of his things into the bedroom closest to the master suite. He'd killed as much time as he could, but he'd run out of things to do. There wasn't anything left now but head downstairs and face the music with Sarah.

He wasn't the least bit surprised to find her sitting at the kitchen table, waiting for him.

"Sit," she commanded, pointing to one of the chairs.

Maybe he could postpone the conversation. "I need to go down and check with Zach—"

Sarah's eyes narrowed and she shook her head. "You ain't goin' nowhere till we have a talk."

It took everything Chance had to keep from squirming under her harsh glare. Some men would have fired Sarah a long time ago for talking to them the way she did him. But Chance knew she was more bark than bite. And besides, she'd been more of a mother to him in the past few years than his own mother had been before she took off with that banker from Boise.

"Yes, ma'am," he said, settling himself in the chair she indicated.

"How on God's green earth did you manage to get yourself hitched up to Mike Lassiter's daughter?" Sarah asked, cutting right to the heart of the matter.

Chance told her what he remembered of the events leading up to, and after, the night in question. He finished by adding, "And when I called the chapel, they confirmed that we're legally married." He paused, swallowed hard, then added, "Since we were both pretty out of it, we…uh, weren't exactly careful. She might be pregnant."

Sarah rolled her eyes and let loose with a heavy sigh. "Have you lost what few brains the good Lord gave you?"

Chance ran a hand across the back of his neck. "I've asked myself the same question ever since I found our marriage license. But fate threw us into this for a reason, and I think it's best to see if we can make it work."

He knew he wouldn't have to explain himself further.

Sarah was superstitious by nature, and a firm believer in destiny and signs. Hell, the woman wouldn't even consider driving out of the yard without her lucky silver dollar, or plant a garden until she'd consulted the *Farmer's Almanac* to see if the signs of the moon were right. And each fall she religiously checked the fur on woolly worms to forecast the severity of winter.

Just as he expected, she turned her attention to more important matters.

"Does Mike know about all this?"

"No." Chance stared at his loosely clasped hands. "I got the impression that's the last thing Kristen wants."

Sarah nodded. "I can understand that. They don't make men any more jackass stubborn than Mike Lassiter."

Chance lifted his gaze to Sarah's. "You know, I can't remember ever doing anything to that man, but the few times I've seen him, he's looked at me like I'm lower than a snake's belly in a wagon rut. Do you have any idea why?"

She patted his hands, her eyes sympathetic. "You haven't done a thing, boy." She paused. "Well, not until you up and married his daughter, anyway."

"Then why—"

"It goes back a long way," she said. "Back to the days when your daddy and Mike traveled the rodeo circuit together."

"They were on the road together?" he asked, astonished. This was the first he'd heard of it. "What happened?"

Sarah shook her head. "That was a long time ago, and it's not my place to spread gossip. But rest assured, it ain't your fault."

Chance stared at the normally outspoken woman for

several long seconds. From the wistful sound of her voice, he could tell Sarah had firsthand knowledge of what had taken place between the two men. "You want to fill me in?" he asked, impatience beginning to claw at his gut.

Sarah shook her head. "I told you, it's not my place to carry tales." She rose from the table. "But be warned, boy. When Mike Lassiter finds out you married his daughter all hell's gonna break loose. He'll show up here with fire in his eyes and brimstone on his breath."

Chance knew better than to press for more information. Sarah had said all she intended to on the subject. And that was that.

As he rose from the chair and shrugged into his jacket, Chance thought about a visit from the mighty Mike Lassiter.

Instead of dreading the confrontation, Chance decided he'd welcome it. He had a few things he'd like to point out to the man. Lassiter was Kristen's father for goodness' sake. Instead of her being afraid of him, he should be the one person she could turn to for support at a time like this.

Chance walked out of the house and headed for the barn. He'd like to keep the peace between the two of them for Kristen's sake. But he had no qualms about what he'd do if the man tried to intimidate her again. His hands balled into tight fists. When Lassiter showed up here at the Sundance, Kristen had nothing to fear.

Kristen lay in the king-size pine bed, staring up at the ceiling. She turned to look at the clock and groaned. The minute hand had barely moved. Exhausted from the trip, she'd fallen asleep right after Sarah had shown her to Chance's room. But that had been almost four hours ago, and for the last two, she hadn't so much as batted an eye.

It was just too quiet. In Dallas, she'd been lulled to sleep by the constant hum of traffic and the noise of a city teeming with life. Here, in the country quiet, the most she could hope to hear was the occasional bawling of a calf trying to find his mother or a coyote howling at the moon.

"Oh, stop lying to yourself," she muttered.

She knew exactly why sleep eluded her. She was in Chance's bed, absorbing the scent of the man she'd shared the most passionate night of her life with. She only wished she could remember what that night had been like.

A tear slipped from the corner of her eye to trail down to her hair. The first time she'd ever made love, the one and only night she'd given her virginity to a man, and she'd missed it. She couldn't remember one single detail. All she knew for certain was that it *had* happened. Of that there was no doubt. The soreness in her lower body yesterday morning attested to the fact that she'd been completely and thoroughly loved.

A shiver of longing slithered up her spine, and she gripped the sheets with both fists. Her mind may not be able to recall the events of her wedding night, but her body apparently remembered it in vivid detail. And if the tingling sensation in her lower belly was any indication, her body wanted it to happen again.

Throwing back the covers, Kristen got up, shoved her feet into her slippers and walked across the room to where her silk robe lay on a huge, plush armchair. Thrusting her arms into the sleeves, she headed for the stairs. She couldn't spend another minute in that bed without losing what little sanity she had left. Maybe if she found something to read she'd be able to relax enough to doze off for a few hours.

She tiptoed past several closed doors, wondering if Chance was inside one of the rooms, his marvelous body sprawled across the bed, the sheet riding dangerously low on his lean hips. The vivid images of awakening next to his nude body in Las Vegas, of him standing in his briefs, completely unashamed of his arousal in their motel room just this morning, came rushing forward.

Kristen groaned and hurried to the stairs. It was best she didn't know what had happened on her wedding night. Memories of the last two mornings were enough to send her into total meltdown. What would happen if she actually remembered making love with Chance?

At the bottom of the stairs, she paused for a moment to get her bearings, then set off down the hall toward the study Sarah had pointed out earlier in the day. If she couldn't find a book on land management or conservation techniques to bore her into falling asleep, she'd read the dictionary or the phone book—anything to take her mind off her temporary husband and the way he made her feel.

The dim light filtering through the windows from the dusk to dawn light outside made navigating the hall easy, and she found the study in no time at all. No sooner had she turned the knob on the closed door than it swung wide and strong arms reached out to haul her into the pitch-black room. Her heart shot up into her throat as the door slammed shut behind her and she found herself pinned against a wall.

Her startled cry set the dogs outside to barking.

"Sh, sweetheart, it's only me," Chance said, his warm breath stirring the hair at her temple.

His low, sexy baritone sent tiny shivers of sheer delight up and down her spine. She drew in a sharp breath. The clean masculine scent that had driven her from the bed filled her senses. The firm muscles beneath his chambray shirt flexed beneath her palms as he shifted his position to settle her against him. Her hands felt as if they'd been scorched from his heat, and her toes curled, uncurled and curled again inside her fluffy bunny slippers as his strong arms held her firmly against him.

When her heart finally left her throat to settle back down into her chest, it was racing, but not from being startled. Far from it.

She wasn't sure where she found the strength to push away from his disturbing embrace, but she did. "You just took ten years off my life," she said, hoping he'd think her breathless tone was due to being frightened. "What on earth are you doing in here in the dark? And why did you drag me in here with you?"

His low chuckle sent another wave of goose bumps shimmering across her skin. "Slow down, sweetheart."

She started to put some much-needed distance between them, but he stopped her. "Be careful. There's a pan of clearing agent to your right."

It took a moment for what he'd said to register. "A pan of what?"

"Clearing agent," he answered patiently. "I'm developing the rolls of film I took at the finals. This is my dark room."

"I thought Sarah said this was the study."

"Nope. That's across the hall."

"When I opened the door, did I ruin the pictures?" Kristen asked as understanding dawned.

"We'll just have to wait and see," he said, sounding vague.

He set her away from him, and she heard him moving around the tiny room. His hand brushed her breast as he reached for something, and she felt as if she'd been branded. The complete darkness added to the intimacy of the small space, and Kristen was relieved that Chance couldn't see her face. If he could, she knew beyond a shadow of doubt that he'd be able to tell just how much he affected her.

She needed to get out of the close confines and put distance between them, but she didn't want to spoil the film. "Is it safe to leave?" she asked.

His big body bumped into her, bringing them into full contact. "Sorry, sweetheart," he said, his hands coming to rest on her waist.

Kristen wasn't sure if he meant she couldn't leave without ruining the film, or whether hc apologized for running into her. At the moment, it didn't matter. The heat of his skin where they touched, the feel of his hands holding her against him, and his low sexy drawl were playing havoc with her good sense.

"Chance, please—"

"Please what, sweetheart? What do you want?"

She swallowed hard. What she wanted was exactly what she couldn't have. Before she managed to find her voice, his hands slipped from her waist to caress her back and pull her to him.

"Want to hear what I want?" he asked, his mouth moving against her forehead.

Beyond the capacity for speech, Kristen found herself nodding.

His low chuckle had to be one of the sexiest sounds

she'd ever heard. "I want to kiss you, Kristen." He gently ran his finger from her ear to touch her lips. "And I want you to kiss me back."

Her knees threatened to buckle. "I...uh, don't think that would be a good idea."

"Probably not in this tiny space," he agreed. His finger traced the outline of her mouth. "But we don't always do what's best, do we?"

"No."

"Would you stop me if I kissed you?" he asked, his voice taking on a rough quality that sent heat streaking through her veins.

Her mind said yes, she would call a halt to it. But instead of saying as much, she shook her head. "No, I won't stop you."

She heard a groan rumble deep in his chest, then his lips covered hers with such tenderness it brought tears to her eyes. As his mouth moved over hers, something deep inside of her seemed to open up like a flower to the bright spring sun. Warmth flowed to every cell in her being and tiny sparkles of light flashed behind her closed eyes.

When he outlined her lips with his tongue, her mouth opened and he slipped inside. His hands stroked her back, then slid down to cup her bottom and draw her to him as he stroked and tasted her. The feel of his arousal pressing against her lower belly turned the tingling she'd fought from the moment she'd awakened in his arms in Vegas into pulsing jolts of electrified desire.

The sound of her own moans penetrated the sensual haze surrounding her. "Chance, let me go," she said, hardly recognizing her own voice. The pictures be damned. She had to get out of there before she did something stupid.

Chance loosened his hold at the desperation he heard in Kristen's voice. Pulling from his arms, she yanked the door open and ran from the room as if the hounds of hell chased her.

What had he been thinking? He'd told himself to take things slow, that pushing for too much, too soon, would only scare her away. But when she'd let him kiss her, his good intentions had flown right out the window. And that's something that had never happened before. Never in his entire life had he gotten so wrapped up in the moment with a woman that he lost all sense of reason.

He scratched at the day-old growth of beard covering his jaw. He'd finished the developing process just before she opened the door, and when she asked if she could leave without affecting the quality of the pictures, he should have told her yes. She'd have walked out, closed the door, the kiss would have never happened and she wouldn't be afraid of him jumping her bones every time they got within spitting distance.

He blew out a harsh breath as he switched on the safe light, bathing the room in a muted red glow. If he wanted things to work out, he'd better watch his step.

Removing the rolls of film from the clearing agent, he pulled them through a scissorlike squeegee, then clipped the strips to a line for drying. As he stood staring at the small frames, he swallowed hard.

There wasn't one single picture of the actual awards ceremony on any of the rolls he'd developed. Every image on every one of the long strips was of Kristen. And most of them had been taken before he'd accepted that first glass of champagne.

Where was the ice maiden? The one with her hoity-toity nose in the air? His lens certainly hadn't captured that side of her. The woman whose image dominated the rolls of film had a soft, sexy look about her that brought every one of his male instincts to full alert.

He shifted from one foot to the other in an effort to ease the sudden tightness in his jeans. Proceeding at a slower pace might prove more difficult than it sounded.

Five

Chance balanced the tray he held in one hand and knocked on his bedroom door. Nothing. Turning the knob, he eased the door open and glanced at the bed. Fast asleep, Kristen lay with the sheet tangled around her long, slender legs. It looked as if she'd had a restless night. A satisfied smile curved his mouth. That made two of them. After that kiss and the discovery of her image on all the pictures he'd developed, he hadn't slept worth a damn.

He placed the tray on the bedside table, then eased down on the bed beside her. "Kristen, sweetheart, wake up," he said gently.

She murmured his name, snuggled closer to his hand still resting on her creamy shoulder, but her eyes remained closed.

Chance gritted his teeth against the electrical impulses traveling up his arm and spreading through his gut. He'd like nothing better than to stretch out beside her, pull her into his arms and make love to her for the rest of the day—to prove to her how good they could be together. But the steamroller approach just wouldn't cut it with Kristen.

He'd done a lot of thinking while he tossed and turned last night in that bed next door, and he'd come to the conclusion that she deserved the works. She might be his wife, but there hadn't been any sort of courting that led up to their marriage. No flowers. No tenderness. No romance.

Women liked those things. Needed them. That's why he'd cornered Sarah first thing this morning and asked if they had one of those fancy trays used for serving breakfast in bed. She'd looked at him as if he'd sprouted another head when she told him no. But she had helped him rummage around in the cabinets to come up with a reasonable substitute.

Chance frowned as he looked at the metal tray with the Bronc Busters logo painted on it. He had no idea where it came from, and he wished it could have had something like a flower on it instead of a long-neck beer bottle, but it would have to do for now.

When Kristen stirred, Chance gulped back a groan. The sheet had slipped to her waist and her pink silk nightgown, draping her beautiful breasts, left no doubt as to the size and shape of her nipples. His mouth went as dry as a desert in a drought.

Unless he wanted her waking up to find him sitting there hard as a rock and ogling her like a teenage boy in a girls' locker room, he'd better get his mind off sex and back on the business of romance. Grabbing the glass of orange juice from the tray, he gulped down half the contents to moisten the cotton coating his mouth.

He gently nudged her shoulder once again and prayed that she'd wake up this time. "Kristen."

"Just five more minutes."

"Sweetheart, I have breakfast for you."

Her eyes popped open. "What are you doing in here?" She jerked the sheet up to her chin.

"I brought you breakfast." He couldn't believe he was jealous of a bedsheet, but the way she clutched it to her made him wish she'd hold him that tightly.

He reluctantly left the bed, retrieved her robe, then handed it to her to put on. There, that should prove to her that his intentions were honorable.

"Thank you, but I don't eat breakfast," she said, sitting up to stuff her arms into the sleeves.

"That's something that will have to change." He reached behind her to prop the pillows against the headboard. "I bought a couple of books on pregnancy and they said good, balanced meals are important for you and the baby right now."

She rolled her eyes. "Will you cut that out? It's too early in the morning for you to start that again."

He ignored her protest, sat back down on the side of the bed and reached for the tray. "I wasn't sure how you'd like your eggs, so I had Sarah scramble them. I hope that's all right."

When she said nothing but continued to glare at him, he smiled. "Not a morning person, huh?"

Chance sat the tray across her legs and picked up the fork lying on top of a paper cocktail napkin. He wished they'd had cloth ones, or even some that were dinner-size. But meals around the Sundance weren't fancy affairs and he'd been surprised to find any at all.

"Just try a bite," he said, spearing a forkful of fluffy yellow eggs.

"Go away."

"Not until you eat something."

She huffed out an exasperated breath. "All I ever have is black coffee."

"Not anymore, sweetheart."

She looked as if she wanted to tear his head off and shout down his neck. "And why not?"

He carried the fork to her lips. "Caffeine isn't good for the baby."

When she opened her mouth to protest, he took advantage of the situation and slipped the fork inside.

Kristen continued to glare at him while she chewed the bite of egg. When she swallowed, he smiled and nodded. "Now, that wasn't so bad, was it?"

"You are without a doubt the most pigheaded, stubborn, misguided man I've ever encountered." She reached for the juice, then held it up to view the half-empty glass. "I suppose now you're going to tell me that only half a serving of orange juice is the recommended amount?"

Chance cleared his throat. "Uh…no. I got thirsty while I was waiting for you to wake up."

She narrowed her beautiful green gaze on him. "Just how long did you sit here on the side of the bed watching me sleep before you woke me?"

This wasn't going the way he planned. She was supposed to be all doe-eyed over his gesture of serving her breakfast in bed, not looking at him as if he were last week's roadkill.

Deciding to ignore her question, he readied another bite of egg. "After you finish eating, we'll take a walk and I'll show you around the ranch. Walking is good exercise when you're expecting."

Her stormy gaze never left his, but when he held the

fork close to her lips, she automatically opened her mouth. He smiled. "Take a drink of milk."

"I don't like it."

"That'll have to change, sweetheart. You'll need extra calcium now."

"I'll take a supplement," she said stubbornly, then shook her head. "Stop that. You're confusing me."

"Good," Chance said, smiling. He offered her a piece of toast. To his satisfaction, she took a bite without stopping to argue. "You're more agreeable when you're not thinking." He reached for the glass of milk. "Now, take a drink and see if it doesn't taste better than you remember."

"No."

"I promise if you take one sip, I'll shut up about it."

"Oh, for heaven's sake," she said, taking the glass from him and gulping down a large amount. She made a face and shuddered. "Now will you take the rest of this away and leave me alone?"

"Take what away?"

Kristen glanced down at the gaudy tray. The plate was completely empty and there wasn't so much as a crumb of toast left.

"Now, see, that wasn't so bad," Chance said, picking up the cocktail napkin with women in pink bikinis printed on it.

When he reached up to hold her chin in one hand while he wiped her mouth with the paper napkin, her gaze locked with his and her breath caught. She'd never thought of the chin as being an erogenous zone, but the feel of his callused palm on her skin made her heart thump against her rib cage and her blood flow through her veins like warm honey.

"You're beautiful when you first wake up," he said,

his blue eyes darkening to navy. He took the tray from her lap and placed it on the bedside table, then reached out to take her into his arms. "I'm going to kiss you good morning, Kristen."

"That's not a good idea." She wished she'd sounded more convincing, but with his strong arms wrapped around her, his warm breath stirring the hair at her temple, she was lucky to form words at all.

"I think it is," he said, his lips pressing tiny kisses from her ear to the hollow of her neck. "We belong together. And I fully intend to prove it to you every chance I get."

She tried to keep from responding to his words, the feel of his mouth on her sensitized skin. If she had any sense, she'd get up, get dressed and get off the Sundance Ranch as fast as her trembling legs would carry her. But instead of pushing him away, Kristen found her arms circling his broad shoulders.

"What makes you think we should stay together?"

"Fate, sweetheart." He nibbled his way across her collarbone. "We wouldn't have gotten married without it."

"We got married because you were drunk and I had a reaction to medication."

He kissed his way from her shoulder to her jaw. "I've been on benders before, sweetheart, and never woke up the next morning with a wife." His lips hovered over hers. "In fact, you're the only woman I've ever spent an entire night with."

Kristen's clouded mind slowly processed that bit of information. How was she supposed to think clearly with his hands caressing her skin, his smooth, sexy drawl lulling her?

"Oh, surely—"

"Nope."

His warm breath feathered over her cheek a moment before his lips settled against hers, and she ceased to think at all. The tingling sensations she was beginning to associate with Chance's touch threaded their way through her limbs, down her body and coiled into tight ribbons of desire in her lower belly.

He tightened his arms around her, and Kristen felt herself being lowered from a sitting position to lie on the bed. When he stretched out beside her and pulled her to him, it crossed her mind to stop him. But only briefly. His tongue tracing her mouth, then dipping inside to stroke, tease and coax, chased away any and all protests. The man's kiss was absolutely lethal.

Threading her fingers through the hair at the nape of his neck, she held him to her. She knew she shouldn't, but she wanted more. Much more.

When he groaned, Kristen realized that somewhere along the way, he'd allowed her to take control of the kiss. He was letting her set the pace and decide how far things would go.

Shivers of feminine power skipped through her, and when he withdrew his tongue, hers followed to enter his mouth. He tasted of orange juice, and pure male desire. She wasn't exactly sure what she was doing, but rewarded by his groan of pleasure and the hard bulge of his erection against her thigh, she figured Chance didn't mind. The knowledge that she could arouse a man to this extent—without even trying—made her feel more desired than she'd ever felt in her life.

He slowly moved his hand from her hip, along her side, dipping at the curve of her waist, cupping the swell of her breast. His thumb circled over the silk covering her nipple, and Kristen shivered from the intense impulses traveling straight to her womb.

The continuous ringing of the phone on the bedside table finally penetrated the thick passion that surrounded her. Pushing against Chance, she drew her robe together. How far would she have let things progress if they hadn't been interrupted?

"Isn't Sarah going to answer that?" She hardly recognized her own voice.

Chance stared down at her for several long moments, his blue eyes blazing with unsatisfied desire. "Sarah left for Amarillo right after she fixed breakfast." He sat up, swung his legs over the side of the bed, then yanked the receiver from the cradle. "Sundance."

Kristen sat up in time to see his eyebrows shoot up a moment before a deep frown creased his forehead. Whoever was on the other end of the line was not delivering welcome news, nor did it appear to be anyone Chance wanted to talk to.

"That's right," he growled. "We were married three days ago."

A sense of impending disaster settled over her. "Who is it?" she whispered, afraid she already knew.

Chance turned to mouth "Your father," and Kristen felt the blood drain from her face and her heart begin to hammer against her rib cage. How on earth had Mike found out? When she'd faxed her report to him she'd been very careful not to arouse suspicions that her trip to the Panhandle was anything more than a vacation.

"No. I won't do that."

With each passing second she could see Chance's jaw muscles tighten further, his frown deepen to a scowl.

"If Kristen wants to go to Dallas, I won't stop her. But it's her choice. I'm for damned sure not going to send her back just because you say to." He listened for a minute, then snarled, "Look, Lassiter, I don't give a damn what you say to me, but you're not talking to my wife until you calm down."

Kristen gasped. Very few people had the nerve to cross Mike, let alone talk to him in such basic terms. He would be livid.

But her respect for Chance rose several notches. He was going to leave the choice up to her. That's something Mike had never done.

"You do that," Chance said, slamming the receiver back onto the cradle. He took a deep breath to calm himself before his gaze met hers. "He'll be here tomorrow."

Kristen's stomach churned. "How did he find out?"

Chance braced his forearms on his knees and stared down at his clenched fists. "The other day when I went down to check you out of the hotel, the video of our wedding hadn't arrived. I told the desk clerk to have it delivered here. But it looks like someone got their wires crossed." He raised his gaze to meet hers. "They sent it to Sagebrush Boots."

"Oh, great." Kristen covered her face with both hands. She felt as if the world had come crashing down on her shoulders. Mike had watched their wedding video—a tape she hadn't seen of a wedding she didn't even remember. "What did he say?"

"He wants me to send you home so he can start annulment proceedings immediately." Chance cupped her face with his large hands. "I meant it when I told him it wasn't for either one of us to tell you what to do." He paused, then added, "If you want to go, I won't stop you, Kristen. But like I told you before, this is a responsibility I intend to take very seriously. I'd like for you to stay until we find out if there's a baby."

Kristen considered what Chance said. Unlike Mike, Chance was quietly requesting that she stay—giving her the opportunity to decide what *she* wanted to do. He'd stated his wishes, but the decision was all hers.

Before she could answer, he rose from the bed, picked up the tray and headed for the door. Turning back to face her, his slow grin made her tingle all the way to her toes.

"But I have to warn you, sweetheart. I'm pulling out all the stops. I'm going to convince you that staying married to raise our baby is the right thing to do."

"But if I'm not—"

"Doesn't matter. Fate means for us to have a baby together. If there isn't one now, I promise there will be." He winked. "Now, get dressed and meet me down by the barn. I want to show you around the ranch."

Kristen stared openmouthed at his retreating back. The man had a one-track mind and he certainly didn't suffer from a lack of confidence.

Chance stood in front of his men, the clipboard in his hand forgotten. He wondered what Kristen would think of them. They sure were an odd mix of age and personalities. But he couldn't ask for a better crew of wranglers. He'd lay his life on the line for any one of them, knowing they'd do the same for him.

"Zach and Joaquin said they saw her while we were in Las Vegas," Spider Evitts said. The oldest and most serious of the bunch, Spider admitted to being in his late thirties, but standing well over six feet and weighing in at a hefty two hundred and fifty pounds, nobody wanted to argue that they knew he was looking long and hard at fifty. "Is she as purty as they let on?"

"She sure is," Chance said proudly.

His grin teasing, Joaquin Morales rocked back on his

heels. "*Por Dios.* If I didn't have Maria waiting on me at home, I'd have given the boss a run for his money with the *señorita.*" Every one of them knew the man was spouting hot air. Joaquin was hopelessly in love with his wife and had been since they were in grade school.

"It's *señora* now," Chance reminded Joaquin.

Harley Tucker spat a stream of tobacco juice close to the toe of Zach's boot and laughed. "Well, the way I see it, now that the boss here has joined the ranks of the blissfully hitched, that just leaves Zach ridin' the high lonesome."

Zach Davis, leaning against the rails of the corral fence, shook his head. "Don't you go gettin' any ideas about havin' Becky fix me up with some little gal, Harley. The last time Spider's wife tried that, I spent six months dodgin' a marriage license and the preacher."

Grinning, Chance clapped Zach on the back. "If you get too lonely, we'll all chip in and take out an ad in the Find-a-Friend section of the newspaper."

"You'd better not," Zach warned, his own smile confident. "I've got enough on every one of you guys to make big trouble with your women."

"I don't see as how you have a thing on me," Harley said, sending another stream of tobacco juice to join the first. It landed mere inches from the toe of Zach's boot. "I ain't done nothin' I can think of."

Zach grinned. "I can always tell Becky you're still chewin' that nasty stuff."

Harley paled. "She'd stretch my hide out to dry."

Zach nodded and turned to Chance. "And I can tell that new wife of yours about that night you and me got liquored up at the Bucket of Suds and—"

"I get the point," Chance said good-naturedly. "No ads in the newspaper."

Joaquin pointed to a spot behind Chance. "Looks like Señora Miller is here for a visit."

Chance turned to see his sister's truck bounce down the road leading into Sundance Valley. Handing his clipboard over to Zach, Chance grinned. "Looks like you're in charge of getting the stock ready for Del Rio."

Zach nodded and took the chart from Chance. "Okay, boys. Let's get to work."

Chance watched the men head for the holding pens and listened to his head wrangler assign them to the necessary chores of getting stock ready for another rodeo while he waited for Beth to pull the dually to a stop beside him. No sooner had she parked the truck than the passenger door flew open and his niece and nephew spilled out like a couple of roping calves from the starting chute.

"Uncle Chance, did you get the pumpkins?" Cody called, launching himself into Chance's outstretched arms.

"Sarah's gone into Amarillo to get them now," Chance said, lifting the boy into a bear hug. "She should be back any time."

"Unca Chance, me, too," Annie said, her dark blond curls bouncing as she ran toward him.

Chance set Cody on his feet and reached down to swing his three-year-old niece up onto his arm. "How's my best girl?"

"I falled off my horse," Annie said solemnly, pointing to a small bandage on the back of her hand. "But Daddy kissed it and made it better."

Chance raised a brow in question as his pregnant sister, Beth, waddled up to join them. "She slid off Mr. Pickles last night when Steve led him back to the barn," she whispered, referring to Annie's ancient pony.

Cody rolled his eyes. "Annie didn't get cut or nothin', but she wouldn't stop howlin' till they put a cartoon bandage on her."

Beth reached out to affectionately ruffle her nine-year-old son's tobacco-brown hair. "I remember when you were smaller, we did the same for you."

"Wanna kiss my boo-boo, Unca Chance?" Annie asked, sticking her tiny hand up to his mouth.

He chuckled and pressed his lips to the pink strip of plastic. "And how did Steve fare through all this?"

"Dad was ready to take her to the doctor until Mom put that bandage on her and she stopped cryin'," Cody said, grinning.

Chance laughed as he put his arm around his sister's shoulder and steered the group toward the house. His brother-in-law's concern for his wife and children was legendary. But Chance couldn't fault Steve Miller one damned bit for being overly protective. Chance was looking forward to being the same way with Kristen and their kids.

"Let's go into the house," he said. "I've got a surprise for you guys."

Kristen stood at the bay window in the kitchen, looking out to where Chance stood, giving orders to his hired hands. She watched him turn to one of them and laugh at something the man said. She couldn't get over the good-natured camaraderie he shared with them. It was so different from the working relationship Mike had with his employees.

Other than his handpicked "yes" men, she doubted Mike Lassiter ever talked to anyone who worked for him. If he did talk to a lesser employee, it was more likely than not that the underling had done something to incur

Mike's wrath and was being called on the carpet for dismissal. Kristen had never known the man to praise anyone for anything.

No, that wasn't right. Since deciding that Spencer Dirkson would be the perfect husband for her, Mike hadn't been able to say enough about Spencer's good qualities. There had even been times when she'd wondered if Mike was trying to convince her, or himself, of Spencer's virtues.

But she'd never marry Spencer no matter how much Mike praised him. She didn't love the man, and the approval she so desperately craved from Mike wasn't something that could be attained through a bartered marriage.

Gazing at Chance, she shook her head. Being married to a man she didn't even know wasn't the answer, either. Especially one her father despised.

Just as she started to turn from the window to join Chance outside, the powerful growl of an approaching vehicle caught her attention. A large, dual-axeled pickup truck pulled to a stop close to the barn, and a very pregnant blond woman, a young boy and a little girl got out of the cab.

Kristen watched Chance catch the boy as he hurled himself into Chance's outstretched arms. Her curiosity increased when he set the child on his feet, then reached out to pick up the tiny girl. No sooner had he swung her up to sit on his forearm than she held her hand to his lips for a kiss.

Chance put his free arm around the woman's shoulders and Kristen's breath caught. As they approached the porch, the sheer joy on Chance's face was undeniable. He looked proud enough to be the children's father.

Disappointment ran through her as she tried to remember if she'd ever heard anyone mention him having children. Even though the possibility was too remote to be worth considering, she'd thought the baby they might have created the other night would be his first. So, why did the thought of him having children with another woman cause an ache deep inside of her?

When the back door opened and they all entered the kitchen, the boy stopped dead in his tracks to stare at her. Looking confused, he glanced from the woman to Chance, then his head swiveled back to Kristen. "Who's that?"

"Cody, don't be rude," the woman said.

"Sorry," the child muttered.

"Don't worry about it," Kristen said, unsure of what else to say.

The woman within the circle of Chance's arm looked from Chance to Kristen, then back to Chance. "Did we drop by at a bad time?"

"No." Still holding the little girl, Chance walked over to where Kristen stood. She felt the tension in his muscles as he put his arm around her waist, and knew immediately this woman's opinion meant everything to him. "Beth, I'd like you to meet Kristen. My wife."

The woman's jaw dropped and she brought both hands to her open mouth in an effort to cover her obvious shock. "Oh, my God!" Tears filled her eyes. "I can't believe it. After all this time—"

"Mom, are you all right?" the boy asked, his concern bringing him to her side. "Dad said for you to take it easy and not get too excited."

"I'm fine, Cody," the woman said. "Your dad worries too much." Stepping forward, she put her arms around Chance. "I'm so happy for you." She released him, then turned to Kristen. "I'm Beth Miller, this sorry sidewinder's sister.'' She smiled and reached out to hug Kristen. ''Welcome to the family.''

Weak from the relief coursing through her, Kristen hugged Beth back. ''Thank you.''

The baby Beth carried kicked out at the contact. ''Looks like my newest one wants to say hi, too,'' Beth said, laughing.

''Looks like it,'' Kristen said. She smiled and rubbed the spot on her own stomach where the tiny foot or elbow had nudged her. What would it feel like to experience that from the inside? Would her abdomen feel as tight to the touch as Beth's had?

Chance bent down to set the little girl on her feet. ''Kristen, this is Annie and Cody,'' he said. ''Our niece and nephew.''

''Howdy.'' Cody wiped his small hand on the seat of his jeans, then extended it to Kristen.

Kristen shook the boy's hand. ''I'm pleased to meet you, Cody.'' She smiled when Annie mimicked her older brother and thrust her tiny hand forward. Bending down, Kristen took Annie's hand in hers. ''You, too, Annie.''

''The kids are going to stay with us for a couple of hours while Beth goes into Amarillo,'' Chance said.

Beth shook her head. ''You two will want to be alone. The kids can go with me.''

''But, Mom, Uncle Chance promised he'd help me and Annie carve a pumpkin for Halloween,'' Cody protested.

''Wanna card a punkin,'' Annie said, her blond curls bobbing as she nodded her head.

''Please let them stay,'' Kristen said, surprised at her own words. She'd never been around children, but Cody and Annie were darling, and she didn't like the thought of disappointing them.

She had firsthand experience of adults making and

breaking promises. When she was small, her mother always offered, but was too ill to help her with things like carving a pumpkin. And the few times Mike had promised to do something with her, he'd conveniently found reasons to cancel their plans at the last minute.

But her baby was going to know that adults did keep promises. At that very moment she made a solemn vow never to promise her child anything she couldn't carry through with.

The grateful smile Chance shot her was absolutely devastating and brought her out of her disturbing ruminations. Her breath caught and her heart fluttered. He really was one of the best-looking cowboys she'd ever laid eyes on.

His gaze lingered on Kristen for several long moments before he turned back to Beth. "Looks like you've been outvoted, little sister. The kids stay here."

"Yippee!" Cody shouted.

"Ippee," Annie said, clapping her little hands.

"Well, if you're sure you don't mind," Beth said uncertainly.

"We don't mind at all," Kristen said.

In truth, having the children as a buffer between herself and Chance would be a welcome relief. The air fairly sizzled whenever they were in the same room and left Kristen feeling completely off balance.

"Sis, before you leave, be sure to give Kristen the name and number of your doctor," Chance said, his arm snaking around Kristen's waist once again. He planted a kiss on the top of her head. "We'll be needing to see an obstetrician in the next week or so."

Kristen gasped and Beth's mouth fell open once again, but Chance didn't appear fazed in the least by their reactions. He just stood there smiling like the Cheshire cat and looking for all the world like a proud father-to-be.

Six

Chance couldn't stop his ear-to-ear grin at the shocked look on the women's faces. But the expression didn't last long. Kristen's elbow in his ribs took care of that.

"Chance, could I speak to you in the study?" she asked tightly. Turning to Beth, she smiled. "Would you excuse us for a moment?"

"Sure," Beth said, shooting him an amused look.

Chance rubbed his side as he followed Kristen down the hall and into his office. Unless he missed his guess, his wife was about to give him his first lesson in matrimonial protocol. Damn; but this was fun.

"Something on your mind, sweetheart?"

"Why in blazes did you tell your sister I needed the name of her obstetrician?" Kristen demanded, propping her fists on her slender hips. Her green eyes sparkled with anger, and her frown told him his answer had better be good.

"Do you know how beautiful you are when you're riled up?" he asked, reaching for her.

"Don't change the subject." She tried to dodge him, but he anticipated the move and pulled her to him.

He used his index finger to ease the line marring her forehead. "You're much too pretty to frown like that."

She wedged her hands between them and pushed on his chest. He tightened his hold.

"Stop that."

"Stop what?"

"Trying to charm your way out of this."

Chance laughed. "I'm just stating the obvious. You are beautiful."

He watched her displeased expression soften, then she shook her head, the frown firmly back in place. "Cut that out. Compliments are not going to get you out of this one. You're in big trouble, cowboy."

"What did I do?" he asked, trying to contain his smile.

"You know damned well—"

"I love it when you talk dirty, sweetheart." He kissed her forehead. "And stop frowning. It'll cause wrinkles."

"You're enough to give anyone wrinkles and gray hair," Kristen shot back.

Chance pulled her closer and kissed the corners of her mouth. "Now, why would you say a thing like that?"

"Because it's true." To his satisfaction, she sounded breathless and not nearly as determined to take a strip off his hide as she had when they'd first entered the study.

Short of air himself, he asked, "Would it help if I said I'm sorry?"

"Yes." She paused, then shook her head as if to clear it. "No."

He slid his hands the length of her back to cup her delightful bottom. She shivered against him. He kissed her temple, then whispered, "Now, what was it you wanted to talk to me about?"

"I...I...can't remember."

"Then let's go help the kids carve their pumpkins," he said, steering her toward the hall. "I just heard Sarah's truck pull up to the house."

Kristen felt dazed as she watched Chance go to work on cutting the tops off two bright orange pumpkins. She'd have to give him one thing. The man was good. If he put his mind to it, she had no doubts he could sell ice to Eskimos, and have them begging to buy it.

She'd been ready to read him the riot act over his ridiculous statement about the obstetrician. But he'd switched the subject, taken her into his arms, and she'd lost every ounce of sense she'd ever possessed. By the time they'd walked out of the study, she didn't have any idea why she'd wanted to talk to him.

"Are you our aunt now?" Cody asked, breaking into her thoughts.

Kristen glanced over the child's head at Chance. He was watching her, his expression guarded. No help there. He looked just as interested in her answer—if not more so—than his nephew.

What was she supposed to say? The truth was, she was pretty unclear about the whole thing herself. If she stayed with their uncle, then she would be their aunt. But she'd only confuse the children if she didn't.

Trying to decide how to answer, Kristen was saved the trouble when Annie's small pumpkin rolled off the table, dropped to the floor and split in half. The little girl immediately threw back her head and screeched at the top of her lungs. Big, fat tears rolled down her chubby cheeks and dripped from the stubborn set of her little chin.

Chance started around the table, but Annie reached for Kristen. "Ant Kissen…my punkin broke."

Kristen hugged Annie close. "It's all right, honey." When Annie laid her head on Kristen's shoulder, she stroked the child's blond curls. The little girl trusted her, accepted her unconditionally, and it warmed Kristen to the depths of her soul. "Uncle Chance had Sarah get a couple of extra pumpkins. Would you like for me to help you carve another one?"

Annie lifted her head from Kristen's shoulder and sniffed. "P-p-pease."

Chance gave her a look that heated her all the way to the marrow of her bones. "I'll get the pumpkin for you and *Aunt* Kristen," he said to Annie, but his gaze never left Kristen.

When he returned from the back porch with the pumpkin, Chance cut the top out and Kristen helped Annie remove the insides. Once the pumpkins had been cleaned out and the eyes, nose and mouth carved, Chance handed out candles to be placed inside.

He lit the wicks just as Sarah walked in. "So what do you think, Sarah?"

Standing back, she surveyed their work. "I'd say those are the best-lookin' jack-o'-lanterns I've ever seen."

"Ant Kissen hepped me," Annie said proudly, patting Kristen's thigh.

"You did most of the work," Kristen said, leaning down to place a kiss on the top of Annie's blond head. It made her feel good to know that the little girl had enjoyed their time together and accepted her without question.

When she straightened, Kristen watched Sarah exchange a look with Chance, saw the woman's nod of approval. Apparently Kristen had passed a crucial point as far as Sarah was concerned.

"How would you kids like to go down to the barn with me?" Sarah asked suddenly. "Patches just had a new batch of kittens."

"Kitties!" Annie hopped from one foot to the other, clapping her hands.

Chance came up behind Kristen and wrapped his arms around her waist as they watched Sarah lead the kids out the door. "Oh, my!" The feel of Chance's warm breath on the back of her neck sent ripples of pleasure coursing through her.

He turned her to face him. "Thank you."

"For what?"

"The way you handled that situation with Annie." He paused to frame her face with his hands. "You're going to be a great mother."

"You think so?" She placed her hand on her flat stomach. She wanted that more than anything, but her mother had died when she was ten and Mike certainly hadn't stepped in to fill the void of a loving parent. "I'm afraid I don't have any experience at nurturing."

"That's understandable. You're an only child and didn't see how your parents cared for a younger brother or sister." His hand covered hers. "But we'll get through just fine. I'm betting you'll know exactly what to do when the time comes." His smile made her stomach drop to her shoe tops, then bounce back into place. "In the meantime, you can practice on me."

His blue gaze held her captive as his lips descended to cover her mouth in the most tender kiss imaginable, and she didn't even think to protest. Her legs felt as if rubber bands had replaced muscle when his tongue teased her to open for him, and she found herself clinging to him for support.

Just when she thought she'd melt in a pool at his feet, Chance broke the kiss. Resting his chin on the top of her head, he took several deep breaths before he spoke. "Are you ready to take that tour of the ranch?"

"Y-y-yes," she finally managed to say. "I…uh, need to get my jacket." What she needed was time to compose herself. If he hadn't ended the kiss, no telling where it would have led.

"Okay." He set her away from him, walked over to the peg rack beside the back door and shrugged into his coat. "I'll go on down and see how the boys are doing with the stock. Meet me down by the holding pens."

"Are you getting ready for another rodeo?"

"Yep." His grin made her heart flutter and her stomach tighten. "But I'm letting the boys handle this one." He winked. "We're still on our honeymoon, Mrs. Warren."

With that parting shot, he placed his Resistol on his head and walked out of the house, leaving Kristen feeling as if her heart might never return to a normal pace.

Chance grinned when he heard the back screen door slam and turned to see Kristen walking across the yard toward him and his men.

"*Dios mío,*" Joaquin murmured, removing his hat. "She's more beautiful than—"

"Down, Don Juan," Zach cut in. "Remember, you have Maria waiting for you at home."

Pride tempered by a twinge of apprehension filled Chance. Kristen *was* beautiful, and she belonged to him. But for how long? She was his wife, she'd be the mother of his child. But that didn't mean she'd stay with him. His mother hadn't stayed with his dad, and they'd *willingly* married each other.

"Damned if you didn't luck out for sure, boss," Harley said, elbowing Chance in the ribs, bringing him back to the present. "Zach and Joaquin was right. That little gal's a hell of a looker."

"Watch your language, boys," Spider warned under his breath. "That there's a real lady. It ain't no wonder the boss roped and branded her."

A sudden thought slammed into Chance as he watched Kristen approach. She was his wife, all right, but she didn't wear his brand. Apparently, when they got married, he hadn't given the matter of a wedding ring a second thought. When Kristen walked up to him, he put his arm around her shoulders and made a mental note to rectify his oversight as soon as possible.

After introducing his men, Chance stood back and watched with amusement as they wiped their hands on the seats of their jeans in order to shake hands with her. Nothing compared to watching a Texas cowhand in the presence of a lady. Manners that were all but nonexistent most of the time were brought out, dusted off and used— if not with finesse—with an abundance of enthusiasm.

"Glad to meet you, ma'am," Spider said, speaking for the group.

"It's nice meeting you all, too," Kristen said, her smile strained.

Chance wasn't sure what the problem was, but he intended to find out.

"Are the trailers loaded, Zach?"

"All except the bulls." Taking the cue, Zach checked his watch. "Come on, boys. We'd better get the lead out.

We need to be leavin' in about an hour if we want to make Del Rio on time.''

"Be careful," Chance said, gazing down at Kristen. "I don't want one of them getting loose with my wife this close." He waited until the men started off toward the bull pens before asking, "What's wrong?"

Kristen took a deep breath. "Mike called."

Just the mention of the man's name set Chance's teeth on edge. "What the hell did he want?"

"Mike's meeting with his lawyers and having the annulment papers drawn up now. He'll have them with him when he arrives tomorrow."

Chance placed his hands on her shoulders and stared down into her troubled green eyes. "Kristen, you know how I feel about all this. I've made no bones about it. I want you to stay and see if we can make this work because of the baby. But the choice is yours. Not mine or your father's. You don't have to sign any papers or make a decision right now. Just remember that."

"I know." She leaned into him. "But Mike isn't going to make this easy."

Chance put his arms around her and simply held her. He didn't know what else to do. He wasn't about to put the pressure on her to stay that Lassiter would put on her to leave. If only the hotel staff hadn't gotten their wires crossed and sent the video to the Sundance instead of mailing it to Sagebrush Boots, Chance would have had time to romance her, give her the opportunity to see they were meant to be together.

"Are you still going to stay until we find out if you're pregnant?" he found himself asking. The other morning in Vegas, she'd said she would, but he wanted to hear her say it again.

She leaned back to gaze up at him. "Yes."

The relief her assurance gave him was short-lived when a commotion down by the bull pens drew Chance's attention. He cursed a blue streak. "Aw, hell, Mangler's loose."

"Mangler? That doesn't sound good."

"It's not." He gave her a push. "Run for that fence over there and don't stop until you get to the top of it." When she hesitated, he yelled, "Run like hell!"

He didn't wait to see if she did what he said. The bull was bearing down on them. Chance had to divert the big Brahman from going after Kristen so she could make it to the safety of the fence. Taking off at a run, he headed straight for the animal. Just as Chance hoped, Mangler changed his course and came after him.

Chance managed to avoid Mangler's first charge by dodging to the side at the last possible moment. Where the hell were Harley and Spider? They were supposed to be mounted on horses with their ropes ready at all times when the bulls were loaded.

Mangler made another pass, just barely missing Chance. The animal turned and stopped a few yards away. He pawed the ground with one heavy hoof as he shook his lowered head and snorted his anger.

Chance stood ready as he awaited the bull's next move. He wished like hell he had on a pair of running shoes or cleats—anything that would give him more traction than the slick-soled boots he wore. But then he hadn't anticipated sparring with Mangler this afternoon. Hell, he didn't make it a habit of playing "chicken" with a two-thousand-pound bull at any time. He left that to the rodeo bullfighters and clowns—a group of men he had the utmost respect for. They'd saved his bacon more than a few times when he'd been traveling the bull-riding circuit. He just wished like hell there were a couple of those painted-up daredevils around now.

With a snort, Mangler charged. Chance might have been successful in avoiding a collision with the pissed-off ton of beef had it not been for his boots. But he knew the moment he tried to sidestep the bull that it was futile. His boot slid in a loose patch of dirt, throwing him off balance and into the animal instead of away from it.

He put his hands out to push off Mangler's head and throw himself out of the way, but his other boot skidded, and when the bull tossed his head, Chance ended up going airborne.

"Son of a bitch," Chance muttered as he flew through the air. "This is gonna hurt like hell."

Kristen turned at the sound of the bull's angry snort to see Chance tossed into the air like a rag doll. When he landed in a heap several feet away, she started toward him. But she'd only gone a few feet before she stopped. The bull had noticed her movement and was headed her way. Caught by the mesmerizing effects of fear, she stood frozen in place. Her mind told her to move and make it quick, but her feet and legs refused to budge.

From the corner of her eye she caught the sight of a horse and rider approaching at a dead run. Then, as if by magic, a second horse and rider appeared on the other side of the ugly animal. Both men swung rope loops over their heads, then threw them a split second apart. As if in slow motion, Kristen watched first one, then the other rope settle around the bull's head and tighten around his thick neck. Jerked to a stop, the beast stomped and snorted as the two cowboys held him in a tight cross tie.

"*Por Dios,* are you all right, *señora?*" Joaquin asked, running up to her.

Kristen blinked. "Uh…yes. I'm fine." She felt dazed by the dizzy rush of adrenaline and fear, but she quickly brushed past the man. "I have to see about Chance."

Starting forward on legs that felt like limp noodles, she quickly gained strength as she ran to Chance's side. Zach was there, his hands checking over Chance's limbs to see if there were any broken bones.

Kristen noticed a few scratches on his cheek and a small bruise developing on his chin, but otherwise he looked none the worse for his brush with the bull. "Chance?"

He groaned and opened his eyes. "I'm getting too damned old for this."

"Are you all right?" She brushed a lock of blond hair from his forehead. "Where does it hurt, darling?"

Her hands trembled as she ran her fingers through his thick hair, searching for any indication that he'd hit his head when he landed. Despite her finding none, Chance groaned as if he was seriously hurt. She glanced past Chance at Joaquin and Zach. "Help me get him to the house."

"Ma'am, he's not—" Zach broke off whatever he was about to say when Chance grabbed a handful of the man's jeans jacket.

"You heard my wife, help me to the house."

Zach frowned and looked as if he wanted to protest, but Kristen didn't give him the opportunity. She'd seen the look that had passed between them and she had plans. "If you won't help me, I swear I'll fire you on the spot. Now, move!"

Chance coughed, then groaned again and closed his eyes. His face looked strained, and she could only imagine how much pain the faker would be in when she got finished with him.

"Do you think you can stand?" Zach asked.

Kristen heard the suppressed laughter in the cowboy's voice, and bit the inside of her cheek to keep from smiling. "I thought you were his best friend?"

"I am," Zach replied, hauling Chance to his feet.

"Then act like it," Kristen snapped. She'd have to apologize to Zach later. But right now, she couldn't let Chance know she was on to him.

"Yeah, act like it," Chance managed to say before he gave into another bout of coughing.

Zach snorted, but didn't comment further.

"Dios mío, we're in for it now," Joaquin said. "Señora Miller is back and here she comes."

"What happened?" Beth called, hurrying down the path from the barn. Sarah was hot on her heels.

"One of those horrible bulls got loose and Chance saved me from being run down," Kristen said, managing to summon tears to fill her eyes. She'd have to apologize to Beth later, too. And Sarah. But, being women, they'd understand. She hoped.

Beth paled. "Chance, do you need Doc McEvers?"

"No." He'd answered his sister, but his eyes never left Kristen. Reaching out to wipe a tear rolling down her cheek, he said, "I just need some rest and I'll be good as new."

Sarah's eyes narrowed a moment before she shook her head. "That brother of yours is too danged ornery to be too bad off, Beth." She patted Kristen's arm. "He'll be fine, honey. He's just shook up a mite. You go on and get him put to bed."

"Take him upstairs to the bedroom," Kristen ordered the men.

Zach and Joaquin supported Chance on either side, then started for the house.

"Where are the children?" Kristen asked. "I don't want them to be upset."

"We left them in the barn where they wouldn't have to witness their uncle making a fool of himself." Beth hugged Kristen. "You do know he's faking, don't you?"

Kristen nodded as she hugged her back. "His coughing didn't quite cover his laughter. But I want to see how far he's going to go with this."

"You have something in mind, don't you?" Beth asked, her blue eyes twinkling.

"Yes."

Beth laughed. "I like you. A lot. You'll be good for that bullheaded brother of mine." She turned to leave. "Thanks for keeping the kids for me. I'll call this evening and you can fill me in on how much you made him squirm."

Sarah patted Kristen's shoulder and chuckled. "You go on and tend to that man of yours. I'll help Beth get the kids' pumpkins and make sure the boys finish gettin' the stock loaded for Del Rio."

Kristen watched Beth and the children get their jack-o'-lanterns into the truck before she headed for the house. She knew she should be upset with Chance for acting as if he'd been hurt when there wasn't a thing wrong with him. But the truth was, she liked being in control. For the first time in her life, a man had let her take charge, and she was going to enjoy every minute of it.

When they entered his bedroom, Chance shrugged away from the two cowboys supporting him. "Okay, boys, I can take it from here."

"The next time you want to play like the wounded hero, you might wanna let me in on it," Zach said, grinning. "You damned near got me fired out there."

"*Sí*, boss," Joaquin said, laughing. "We'd all be looking for jobs if we hadn't figured out what you were up to."

"I'll remember that next time," Chance said, grinning. He sat down on the side of the bed. "Speaking of jobs, you'd better get out there and help Harley and Spider get Mangler loaded up so you can get on the road."

Zach nodded. "We'll see you when we get back next week."

Chance watched the two men leave, then waited for Kristen. He probably should be shot for taking advantage of her concern and causing her to worry. But he'd told her he intended to pull out all the stops to convince her she should stay. He figured now was as good a time as any to escalate his efforts.

Besides, his time was running out. Lassiter would be here first thing in the morning. Maybe if Chance let her give him a little tender loving care now, she'd decide he needed her. Women liked that—being needed. He grinned. He'd told her she could practice taking care of him, and if that meant he had to act as if he'd been hurt to help her discover her nurturing instincts, then that's what he'd do.

"I can't believe they didn't help you get into bed," Kristen said, hurrying into the room.

"They have a job to do, sweetheart," Chance said weakly. He'd better do some damage control or she'd be insisting he fire Zach and Joaquin as soon as they got back from Del Rio. "I told them to go on."

He bent over to remove his boots and groaned. The truth was his back was stiffening up, and past experience told him he'd be sore as hell by morning.

"Here, let me get those for you," Kristen said, turning

her back to him and straddling his leg. She picked up his boot and tugged.

Chance swallowed hard and raised his hands to caress her rear. No. He'd better not. He didn't dare act too frisky or she'd wise up to him. But her cute little bottom bobbing in front of his face while she struggled with his boots was damned tempting. He finally caught her hips with his hands to stop the movement and barely resisted the urge to plant a kiss on the designer label of her jeans.

When she turned back to face him, she apparently took his strained expression for one of pain. In a soft, soothing voice, she said, "Let's get you out of that shirt."

Her slender fingers brushed his chest as she knelt down to work on the snaps. He felt his blood pressure rise. When she pushed the chambray from his shoulders, her nails grazed his skin and his muscles tightened in response.

"Oh, you have a nasty bruise on your shoulder."

"I do?" He glanced at the blue mottling his skin. "I'll survive."

She finished removing the shirt. "I was so distracted I didn't notice this before. How did you get this scar?" she asked, gently touching his left side and the long white line running from his chest around to his back.

Chance felt the familiar stirring below his belt. He had to clear his throat before he could answer without sounding strangled. "I had a run-in with a brindle bull named Bad Attitude a few years back. He won."

Kristen lifted her gaze to his. "Was that when you had to quit riding?"

He nodded. If his life depended on it, Chance couldn't have formed another word. Her touch, the soft feminine scent of her designer cologne, had him so tied in knots he figured he might just be mute from now on.

She pressed a soft kiss to the scar, and he couldn't stop the long, low groan that had been building inside him from the moment she started to take off his boots.

"Oh, Chance, I'm sorry," she said, rising to her feet. "You must feel terrible. Stand up so we can get you out of those jeans and into bed."

Oh, yeah.

If her taking his jeans off turned out to be half as much fun as when she removed his shirt, he decided he'd die a happy man. But he'd better take it slow. If he stood up too fast, he'd give himself away.

When he finally came to his feet, Kristen reached for his belt buckle, her warm fingertips skimming his belly as she worked on the leather strap. He gritted his teeth. She popped the snap at the waistband, and to his heightened senses it sounded as if a cannon went off. He brought his hands up and placed them on her shoulders to keep from wrapping his arms around her. One of her fingernails scraped the teeth of the zipper when she reached for the tab, and he felt himself come to full erection.

Not good, Warren.

In his condition, the zipper could become a lethal weapon if it wasn't lowered carefully. Besides, once his jeans came off she'd see he was way too aroused for a man who was supposed to be injured.

Chance groaned and brushed her hands away from the very spot he'd most like her to touch. "I'm starting to hurt something awful, sweetheart. Could you get me a couple of aspirin while I shuck my jeans?"

"Of course," she said, her smile sympathetic.

When she turned to walk into the adjoining bathroom, he made quick—but careful—work of easing the zipper down and sliding his jeans off. Tossing the bedspread back, he hopped into bed and carefully arranged the covers.

"That was quick," she said when she returned from the bathroom. Handing him two white tablets and a glass of water, she supported his head and shoulders while he downed the pills.

"Thanks." When she turned to leave, he frowned. "Where are you going, sweetheart?"

"I'm going to make an ice pack for your shoulder." Her soft hand comforting, Kristen gently brushed his hair from his forehead. "I'll only be gone a few minutes."

Chance watched her leave. Damn, but he could get used to this. Smiling, he folded his arms behind his head. Now that he was in bed, all he had to do was figure out how to get Kristen to join him.

Happy with the way things were turning out, a sudden thought sent him scrambling from the bed and into the bathroom. He yanked open the medicine chest above the sink to search the shelves. Nothing.

"Damn," he muttered, closing the mirrored door.

When he'd stopped in Gallup to purchase the books on pregnancy he'd decided against buying condoms. Hell, at the time he hadn't intended to seduce Kristen, let alone stay married to her. And if she wasn't pregnant now, he for damned sure didn't want to make her that way. He wanted her to stay with him because it was what she wanted, too, not because she felt that he'd trapped her.

Chance slowly walked back into the bedroom and picked up his jeans. He didn't really expect to find what he was looking for, but on the outside chance…

Seven

Kristen walked into the kitchen, rummaged through the cabinets until she found a self-sealing plastic bag, then went straight to the refrigerator. Opening the freezer door, she grabbed some ice, but instead of filling the bag, she pressed the cold cube to her heated forehead. How much further would Chance carry this ruse? More important, how much more of it could *she* take?

He'd allowed her to take off his shirt, touch the hard muscles of his chest, explore the scar marring his marvelous body. She brought the ice to the hollow of her throat and pressed it against her rapid pulse. Thank the moon and stars above that he'd stopped her when she reached his fly. She could only imagine the kind of shape she'd be in if he had allowed her to take off his jeans.

Have mercy! His impressive arousal had strained at the zipper, the denim pulling tight over his lean flanks. It had taken everything she had to keep from touching him to see if it felt as firm as it looked.

Kristen shivered, but it wasn't due to the ice cube on her skin or the frosty air rushing from the freezer to bathe her flushed face. The plain and simple truth was, she had the hots for her husband.

"Are you lookin' for somethin'?" Sarah asked, walking in from the back porch. She came up behind Kristen to peer into the freezer compartment. "Or are you just gonna stand there till you get frostbite?"

Kristen blinked as she came to her senses. "Uh…no." She reached into the ice bin and began filling the bag with cubes. "I…thought I'd fix Chance an ice pack for his shoulder."

Sarah laughed. "Honey, it's my bet his shoulder ain't the body part that boy needs coolin' off." Her grin wide, she patted Kristen's cheek. "And you're lookin' a mite hot and bothered yourself."

Kristen felt her face heat even more at Sarah's candid comment.

"Ain't nothin' wrong with wantin' to be with your man, honey," Sarah continued. She walked into the pantry. When she returned she held two cans of beef stew. "Now, I'm gonna put this on to simmer for your supper, then I'm takin' off to visit my sister in Amarillo." She grinned, her expression meaningful. "I won't be back till mornin'. Think you can handle fixin' breakfast tomorrow?"

"Sure," Kristen said, her voice a bit unstable.

With Sarah gone, that left her alone with Chance. Not good. Not good at all. How was she ever going to keep her distance with him?

Sarah pulled a saucepan from the cabinet, opened the cans and emptied the contents into the pan. Placing it on the electric burner, she turned back to Kristen. "How much longer are you gonna let him play at bein' hurt?"

More comfortable with this topic, Kristen grinned. "I'm not sure."

Sarah laughed. "Well, if you wanna make him squirm a little more before you tell him you know what's goin' on, I've got an idea."

Kristen liked Sarah more with each passing second. "What have you got in mind?"

When he heard Kristen outside the bedroom door, Chance barely had time to affect a pained expression before she entered. She had a plastic wash pan in one hand and a bottle of what he could only guess to be liniment in the other. The medicated oil he could understand. She'd rub his sore shoulder with that. But what was up with the wash pan?

"Feeling any better?" she asked, walking straight into the bathroom.

"A little." He heard her turn on a faucet, then heard cabinet doors open and close. Now what the hell was she up to? And why did she need water?

Returning, she held the pan full of soapy water and had a towel and washcloth tucked under her arm. She set everything on the bedside table. Her smile sympathetic, she pulled the sheet and blanket down to his waist.

He gulped. Hard.

"After a bath, I'll rub your shoulder."

His mouth went dry. He'd just barely managed to get his body back under control from her undressing him. A sponge bath was the last thing he needed. One touch of her soft hands on his body and there wouldn't be any doubt that he was faking his injuries.

"Uh...I don't think I'm up to a bath, sweetheart."

"Nonsense. It'll help you relax."

Like hell!

"I'm really tired...."

He felt as if someone had punched him in the gut when she smiled down at him. "You don't have to do a thing but lie back and rest. I'll do all the work for you."

His heart pounded against his ribs like an out-of-control jackhammer. He watched her reach into the front pocket of her jeans, remove some kind of bright pink thing and pull her silky auburn hair back to secure it with the fluffy band. It looked as if she meant to get down to some serious business with this bath idea of hers.

It took several swallows to get words past the cotton coating his throat. "You don't have to—"

"Oh, I don't mind," she said, dipping the washcloth into the pan. She wrung out the excess water, then sat down on the bed beside him. "It'll only take a few minutes, and it's the least I can do. You saved my life when you stepped in front of that bull."

"It was nothing." He cleared his throat. "Really."

"Oh, but it was. You put your safety ahead of mine."

"I'm your husband. I'm supposed to protect you."

She smoothed his hair back from his forehead with one hand while she gently ran the cloth over his brow. She slowly drew it down over his cheeks and across his chin, then the column of his neck. Chance never would have guessed any of those areas could excite him. They never had before. But Kristen's touch had him aroused in a whole ton of ways he'd never experienced before.

He caught her hand in his to stop the torture she was putting him through, but she pulled free. Dipping the cloth back into the water, she shook her head. "We aren't finished yet, darling."

When she touched his chest with the warm, damp terry

cloth, Chance felt his lower body jerk with an intensity that felt like he'd been treated to the business end of a cattle prod. Her hand pulling the nubby cloth over his stomach made his muscles quiver and his breath come out in one big whoosh. By the time she finished bathing his arms, he figured he was hot enough to ignite the bedsheets.

She put the washcloth back into the water and patted him dry with the towel. Smiling, she reached for the covers, but before she could pull them down and reveal more than Chance cared to show at the moment, he grabbed her wrists. "I'm really starting to hurt, sweetheart."

Her smile was so damned sweet and caring, it was all he could do to keep from pulling her down beside him. "Now, what kind of nurse would I be if I didn't finish the job?"

Chance closed his eyes and gritted his teeth. It wouldn't take much to finish him off, that was for damned sure. Groaning, he pulled his legs from either side of the covers, careful to keep the bedding bunched up over his groin. One look at that area, and she'd know for sure there wasn't anything wrong with him.

Kristen's brow rose. "Don't tell me you're shy?"

He opened his eyes to glare at her. "You could say that."

"I never would have guessed that of you," she said, wringing out the cloth.

She ran the rag over his shin and knee, then up to the leg band of his briefs. But when she started down toward the inner part of his thigh, he caught her wrist.

"What the hell are you up to, woman?"

"I'm giving you a bath," she said, sounding completely innocent.

Chance let out his pent-up breath. "You take care of everything from my knees down, and I'll take care of the rest later."

"You really are shy." She sounded amazed.

"Yeah," he said, disgusted with himself and the position he'd gotten himself into. "I'm a regular shrinking violet."

"If you say so."

She was either a damned good actress or she really didn't have a clue about the kind of effect she had on him. Either way, by the time she'd finished with his bath, Chance was in pain. But it had nothing to do with any kind of injury.

Apparently, his discomfort was visible.

"You really are hurting, aren't you?"

Oh, yeah.

"Nothing I can't handle," he said through clenched teeth.

Her understanding smile just about turned him wrongside out. "Poor baby. Why don't you turn over and let me massage your shoulders and back?"

He tried to think of a reason not to do as she asked. Her hands caressing him was the very last thing he needed at this point.

"I don't think I can. My back's pretty stiff."

Along with other things.

"All the more reason you need a massage." She picked up the bottle of oil and poured a generous amount into the palm of her hand.

"That's not liniment."

"No. It's lavender body oil. It'll help you relax. Now, turn over."

"Oh, hell," he muttered as he rolled over. "I'll smell

like a damned flower. You're a mighty mean nurse, you know that?''

She leaned down to whisper close to his ear. ''And you're a grouchy patient.''

Her warm breath teased his ear, and when she placed her hands on his back to spread the oil over his muscles, he thought he might explode right then and there. Kneading, rubbing, she worked her way down his spine and along his sides. When she reached the waistband of his briefs, Chance buried his head in the pillow and gritted his teeth so hard, his jaw ached. But her fingers dipping beneath the elastic to spread the oil over his hips and the small of his back had him feeling like the top of his head might come off.

This had turned out to be the dumbest idea he'd ever come up with. He was hurting, all right, but it had nothing whatsoever to do with sparring with Mangler. He wanted—no, needed—her more than he ever had any woman. But by faking injury, he'd boxed himself in. If she found out now that he was perfectly fine, she'd never forgive him.

Kristen watched both of Chance's fists clench the sheet in a death grip as she smoothed the oil over his shoulders and back. She had to give him credit, he was holding up fairly well, all things considered. But she wasn't sure how much longer she could keep up her end of the ruse. Touching his hard muscles, feeling his skin heat as his desire mounted, proved to be a real test of her own endurance.

She might have been able to resist getting caught up in the intense longing caused by touching him if he hadn't let her take control of the situation. For the second time in one day, he was allowing her to be in charge and experience the full extent of her feminine power. And she found that to be a very heady thing.

But she was beginning to suffer almost as much as she figured Chance was. Her heart pounded like a jungle drum, and her blood felt like liquid fire rushing through her veins.

Leaning over, she whispered in his ear, "Aren't you about ready to give up this sham and admit there isn't a single thing wrong with you?"

She felt his body tense a moment before he turned to flip her over on her back and pin her to the mattress.

He stared down at her, a feral gleam in his dark blue eyes. "How long have you known?"

Kristen forced herself to breathe. "Oh, about the time you insisted that Zach and Joaquin help you into the house."

"Then why didn't you say something?"

She laughed. "I wanted to see just how far you'd take your little ruse."

"Do you have any idea how much hell you put me through, sweetheart?" he asked, kissing the hollow at the base of her throat.

She shivered against the tingling sensation gathering in her lower stomach. "You deserved it for acting like you were injured when you weren't."

His grin held a wealth of promise. "Payback time."

Before she could protest, he pulled her beneath the covers, his lips teasing hers with such tenderness, she thought she'd go mad. When he deepened the kiss, Kristen moaned, the sound so filled with longing it surprised even her.

He tugged her T-shirt from her jeans, then slipped his hands beneath the hem of it to explore the newly exposed area. The calluses on his palms sent waves of sheer delight straight to the core of her as he caressed her ribs, the underside of her breasts. His busy fingers made quick work of the front clasp of her bra, and when he kissed his way up from her abdomen to take the peak into his mouth, Kristen thought she'd die from intense need.

Feeling as if she were burning up from the inside out, she pressed her legs together to try to ease the empty ache. As if he knew what she needed, Chance reached down to cup her there, his fingers pressing against the heated denim.

When she started to protest, he covered her lips with his as he released the button at the waistband of her jeans and slid the zipper down. Easing his hand beneath her silk panties, he found and parted her, his finger stroking the taut, sensitive little nub until she bucked against him.

"Easy, sweetheart."

"Chance—"

"Let me do this for you." He placed tiny kisses on her heated skin and murmured assurances as his finger dipped deeper, to stroke her inside.

Kristen didn't have the strength to tell him no as wave after wave of pure desire overtook her. Her stomach tightened with feeling, the unfulfilled ache building to unbearable proportions. Moaning, she clutched at his shoulders.

"Let go, Kristen," he whispered against her breast. "Just let it happen, sweetheart. I've got you and I won't let go. You're safe."

He continued stroking her, his relentless fingers caressing her inner core, the small bud of intense sensations. He was demanding that she give in to the passion that threatened to consume her, to trust that he would take care of her. His mouth found one of her nipples and drew on it deeply, the pull in her womb taking her over the edge and into the shattering realm of pure pleasure.

Chance felt Kristen's feminine muscles tighten, then flex and contract around his fingers as her climax overtook her. Her nails pressing into his skin, she cried out his name. He tightened his arms and held her close as she rode out the storm. His own body throbbed for the same release, but he gritted his teeth and ignored it. This time was for Kristen—for her pleasure, not his.

When she finally went slack, her satisfaction complete, Chance finished undressing them. He slid his hand beneath the pillow, found the small foil packet he'd placed there just moments before she'd walked into the room and, hoping the damned thing wasn't too ancient to be effective, arranged their protection.

Covering her lips with his, Chance once again began to explore Kristen's body, to bring her to the brink with his touch. When he eased himself into position and slipped inside her sweet warmth, Chance ground his teeth at the feel of his wife's tight body surrounding him. He set a steady pace, but her low moan of pleasure snapped his restraint and he ceased to think at all. Nothing mattered but the primitive need to make her his, to fill her with all of himself, to be part of her.

He felt his muscles bunch and coil for the final surge, then blinding light burst behind his closed eyes as tremors racked his body. His explosion went on and on, and when he finally collapsed on top of her, his breathing ragged, he felt lower than dirt. Never before had he ever lost control with a woman and not insured her satisfaction.

Rising up on one elbow to beg her forgiveness, the last thing Chance expected was for her to bury her face in his chest and emit a nervous giggle. "Sweetheart—"

"We shouldn't have done that," she mumbled against his skin.

"Why not?"

Unless he missed his guess, Kristen was embarrassed. He found her reaction endearing, but it was the very last thing he expected. He figured she'd be upset with him for his lack of restraint and finding pleasure ahead of hers, but he never in a million years would have anticipated her being self-conscious. Apparently, it had been a long time since she'd been intimate with a man.

He liked the thought. A lot.

"Kristen, look at me."

"No."

"Sweetheart, are you embarrassed by what just happened?"

She nodded.

He pulled back to look at her flushed face. "It's been a while?"

Her cheeks colored a deeper shade of rose. "You could say that."

Something in her tone made his stomach do a back flip and his apology died in the back of his throat. "Exactly what kind of time frame are we talking here, sweetheart? A year? Two?"

She continued to stare at his chest. "More like twenty-seven."

Chance felt his heart stop, then take off at a gallop. "Are you telling me—"

"Yes." Her voice defensive, she glared up at him. "I was a virgin until our wedding night. You have a problem with that?"

"Hell, no," Chance croaked when he finally found his voice.

An unnamed feeling began to fill his soul. He wasn't

about to analyze its source or put a name to it. It didn't matter. Fate had once again stepped in to reinforce his belief that they should stay together. She'd waited for her husband, and Chance just happened to be that man.

"Why would I complain about being the only lover my wife's ever known?" But a niggling little doubt began to take root. "Sweetheart, I don't recall seeing…I mean, shouldn't there have been a little blood—"

"There wouldn't be," she said, pulling from his arms. She got out of bed and wound the bedsheet around her, blocking his view of her delicious body. "When I was younger, I fell really hard during a gymnastics lesson. I guess you could say that took care of any so-called evidence."

She kept her back to him as she gathered her clothes, and he knew his doubt had hurt her. Leaving the bed, Chance pulled on his briefs, then came up behind her to wrap his arms around her waist. He pulled her against him and kissed her slender neck. "I'm sorry. I'm just a little overwhelmed to find out you've waited all this time."

"If you'll remember, I wasn't exactly myself when we got married." She shrugged one shoulder. "And before that…well, I couldn't be intimate with a man because I was never sure whether it was me or Mike's money they found attractive." She paused. "I'm pretty sure that's why he married my mother. Her family owned Sagebrush Boots."

Chance couldn't believe any man would prefer money or running a company to the treasure of a woman like Kristen. True, there were times when she could send the temperature in the room down at least ten degrees with nothing more than a look. But those were becoming fewer and further apart. The better acquainted he became with his wife, the more he saw of the warm, passionate woman just beneath that aloof facade.

Turning her to face him, he cupped her cheeks with his hands. "I've got my own money, Kristen. I don't want or need anything from your father, except you."

"But—"

Chance shook his head. "Only you and our baby."

He could tell she was having a hard time grasping the concept, so he showed her in the only way he knew how. Lowering his head, he kissed her, allowing her to taste his sincerity, the depth of need she created in him.

Her soft lips opened for his entry and Chance used his tongue to imitate the act of love, to show her how much he wanted her. Every muscle in his body screamed for the physical release that loving her again would bring, but he had to deny himself. He didn't have anything else to protect her. And he didn't want her thinking this was just a ploy to get her back into bed.

Breaking the kiss, he wrapped his arms around her and took deep breaths to try to chase away the uncontrollable urge to do just that. "Maybe you'd better go down and see if Sarah needs help with supper."

"Sarah isn't here. She said to tell you she's gone to visit her sister and won't be back until morning. But she did put some stew on to simmer."

Chance felt a tremendous surge to his groin at her announcement. He'd been counting on Sarah providing a buffer between them until he could get to town to buy more condoms.

"Have you made up your mind to stay with me whether you're pregnant or not?"

"No."

"I didn't think so. Sweetheart, I don't want you taking

this the wrong way,'' he said, bracing his hands on her shoulders. ''But get the hell out of here.''

She searched his face a moment before glancing down at the bulge straining his cotton briefs. When she lifted her gaze back to his face, her cheeks had colored a pretty pink. ''Oh, my.''

''That's right, sweetheart. I want you. Again.'' Chance gritted his teeth against the fresh need sweeping through him. ''Now, get dressed, then go downstairs and check on that stew.'' When she hesitated, he gave her a pointed look, then started for the bathroom. ''While I take a cold shower and freeze my…butt off, you get dressed and get the hell out of here.''

Kristen knocked on the door frame before entering the study. After Chance finished his shower, he'd come downstairs and gone straight to work on something that had to be giving him fits. More than once she'd heard his graphic curses all the way to the kitchen.

Glancing up from the computer, he smiled. The relieved look on his face plainly stated he wasn't the least bit upset by the interruption.

''If you can break away from what you're doing, dinner's ready.''

''Thanks.'' He rose slowly and rubbed his back. ''I'm not getting much done, anyway. I've been performing more 'illegal functions' than anything else.''

''What are you working on?'' she asked, coming around the desk to look at the monitor.

''I'm trying to bring the Sundance into the age of technology.'' He chuckled. ''But it might help if I knew what the hell I'm doing.''

Kristen looked at the pile of papers on his desk, then at the monitor. ''You need to use a tracking program for this part of your business instead of an accounting format.''

''You know how to do this stuff?'' he asked, sounding hopeful.

She nodded as she continued to analyze the data on the screen. ''I have a master's degree in business administration.'' Shuffling through the papers, she glanced up at him. ''I take it you're trying to input your whole operation?''

He nodded and pointed to a book lying on the desk. ''The guy at the computer store said all I had to do was read this and I wouldn't have any trouble setting up my business accounts, breeding records and anything else I wanted to put on there.'' He gave her a disgusted look. ''He lied.''

She grinned and shook her head. ''Well, not exactly. You can do all those things with this program, but the salesman failed to tell you it's not as user-friendly as some of the others.''

''What program would *you* suggest?'' he asked, sounding genuinely interested in what she had to say. ''If you have any ideas on how to make this transition easier, I'd like to hear them.''

Shocked, Kristen stared at him for several long seconds. Chance was asking for her advice? Amazing. Mike never listened to anything she had to say pertaining to business, let alone asked for her opinion.

She shook her head. She'd have to quit comparing Chance to Mike. They were worlds apart. While Mike insisted on holding her down to the traditional female role of his day, Chance was encouraging her to be modern and progressive. He wasn't the least bit threatened by her expertise.

Naming a couple of programs she thought would better

suit his needs, she added, "They're expensive, but I think they'd be well worth the money."

Chance draped his arm over her shoulders. "Sweetheart, I don't care what it costs. If you say that's what I need, then that's what I'll get."

Kristen felt warmed to the depths of her soul. Having a man listen to her and take her advice was quite enjoyable and satisfying.

Turning her to face him, he asked, "Would you mind helping me get this set up and everything organized?"

"I'd love to," she said, thrilled at the idea of finally being allowed to use her degree.

His grin made her insides feel like melted butter. "How would you like to turn off that stew and take a trip into Amarillo? We can grab a steak dinner, go to the software store in the mall, then catch a movie."

She circled his waist with her arms. "Are you asking me out on a date, Mr. Warren?"

"Why, yes, Mrs. Warren," he said, his low, sexy drawl sending tiny shivers of excitement along every nerve in her body. "I believe I am."

Kristen sniffed as she and Chance left the theater. "That was such a good movie."

He tightened his arm around her shoulders and guided her across the parking lot to the truck. "Then why are you crying, sweetheart?"

"I'm not."

"Are, too."

"I never cry." *Where anyone can see.*

"Uh-huh." He used the pad of his thumb to wipe away the tear slipping down her cheek. "You know, there's no reason to be embarrassed with me."

Kristen felt her cheeks heat. "I'm not embarrassed. The sinus infection—"

"Is clearing up."

Shrugging, she sniffed again. "Okay. I was crying. But it's just so touching. Even though the hero died, you know the heroine's love for him will last a lifetime—that he'll stay in her heart forever."

Chance helped her into the truck, then walked around the front to climb into the driver's side and slam the door. "I still can't believe *that* many people would be interested in an eighty-year-old disaster."

"It's going to be a classic."

"It's a chick flick."

She glared at him. "What's wrong with a good love story?"

"Not a damned thing." He eased the truck out into the flow of traffic. "But I like a happy ending."

"How would you have ended the story?"

He didn't even hesitate. "I'd have both of them survive, her mother would come down off her high horse and realize money isn't everything, they'd get married and everyone would sail off into the sunset."

"You've seen too many old westerns," Kristen teased.

"Maybe so. But in the end, the guy always wound up with the girl."

She folded her arms beneath her breasts and shook her head. "In most of those movies the cowboy kissed his horse and rode off alone. The woman was left waving goodbye."

Chance shot her a grin that warmed her all the way to her toes. "I'd kiss you and wave goodbye to the horse."

Feeling more relaxed than she had in days, Kristen laughed. "What kind of cowboy would abandon his horse for a mere woman?"

"A smart one."

"But I'll bet his truck would be a different matter entirely," she teased. It was common knowledge that Texas men and their trucks were inseparable.

"I'd definitely keep my truck," he said, reinforcing the legend. He pondered that for a moment before adding, "But now that you mention it, it might not be a bad idea to check into getting one of those minivans. We'll need something bigger when the baby gets here." He paused. "Unless you'd rather have a sedan or station wagon."

"How do you do that?"

"Do what?"

"Turn everything I say into a reference about a baby or us staying married."

He steered the truck onto the lane leading to the ranch. "Because we're meant to be together, sweetheart. You're the other half of me."

Kristen couldn't have responded if she'd tried. His sincere expression, the strength of conviction in his voice, caused a lump to form in her throat. She'd never had anyone express such a strong desire for her to be part of their life.

And it came as no small surprise that the idea of staying married to Chance and having a baby didn't shake her nearly as much as it had a few days ago. In fact, she found the idea of caring for and loving a child of her own more appealing with each passing day.

But what would Mike do if she stayed with Chance? Could she live with the consequences that decision would cause? Mike wasn't much of a parent, but he was all the family she had left. Could she accept being cut off from her only living relative?

And what if there wasn't a baby on the way? Chance

had convinced himself that she was pregnant, but that didn't make it fact. She glanced at the sacks between them. Besides the computer shop, they'd visited several stores in the mall, one of which had been a department store. The pregnancy test she'd purchased while Chance looked at camera equipment should prove one way or the other within the next day or two whether there was a child.

Would he still want them to stay married if the test turned out negative? Could he look at her as more than an obligation—the consequence of a reckless night? He'd said as much, but did he really mean it? Her own father always treated her as a liability, why would an accidental husband be any different?

Then there was the matter of love. Chance had talked of fate, babies and staying married, but not once had he mentioned falling in love. She wondered if he might have some misguided, old-fashioned male belief that it was the responsible thing to do—to protect her reputation.

"Looks like we have company," Chance said, breaking into her disturbing thoughts.

He steered the truck into the ranch yard and stopped next to a shiny black sedan. The driver's door opened immediately and a tall bear of a man stepped out to glare at her through the passenger side window of the truck.

Kristen's breath caught and her heart pounded hard against her ribs. She'd never in her entire life seen Mike Lassiter look more furious.

Eight

Chance didn't like the turn of events one damned bit. He'd wanted more time with Kristen, wanted the bond developing between them to grow stronger before Lassiter arrived. But time had run out. Nothing left to do now but get the showdown over.

Chance got out of the truck and ignored the man staring daggers at him as he walked around to open the passenger door. When Kristen took the shopping bags, he cut her a sideways glance. The apprehension etched in her beautiful face tore at his gut.

Framing her face with his hands, he smiled. "It's going to be all right, sweetheart."

"Get your filthy hands off my daughter, Warren," Lassiter growled.

Kristen paled. "Mike—"

"Let me handle this," Chance said, putting his arm around her. When they turned to face the man, Chance extended his right hand. "Welcome to the Sundance, Mr. Lassiter."

Lassiter ignored the gesture. "Get your luggage, Kristen. I'm taking you home."

"She is home," Chance said, sizing up the gray-haired man in front of him.

Mike Lassiter was close to the same height as Chance's own six feet, but outweighed him by a good forty pounds. Taking into account the twenty-five year difference in their ages and the man's softer life-style, Chance figured he would have a distinct advantage if it came down to a fight.

"Kristen, do as I said," Lassiter ordered. "I've got two rooms reserved at the Ambassador in Amarillo. Tomorrow we'll take the corporate jet back to Dallas and be there by the time the courthouse opens."

Chance felt the tension in Kristen's slender shoulders increase. But to her credit, when she answered the man glaring at her, her voice was steady and calm. "No, Mike. It's late, and I'm very tired. We'll discuss this in the morning after you've calmed down." Turning to Chance, she kissed his cheek. "I'm going on up to *our* room."

When Kristen walked past him to enter the house, her father looked as if she'd slapped him. It was all Chance could do to keep from shouting in triumph. He wasn't sure if his elation was due to what he'd bet to be Kristen's first act of standing up to her father, or the fact that she'd referred to the bedroom as *theirs*.

At the moment, it didn't matter. Things were going his way and he wasn't about to question his good luck. He shoved his hands into his jeans pocket, his fingers coming into contact with the polished stone. As long as he had his lucky agate, he figured he couldn't lose.

"I'll be back first thing in the morning for my daughter, Warren." Lassiter looked a little less sure of himself, a little more agitated.

Rocking back on his heels, Chance came to a decision. No matter what he thought of the man, Lassiter was Kristen's father. For her sake, if for no other, Chance wanted there to be some semblance of peace between the two of them.

"It's a long drive back to Amarillo. You might as well stay here tonight."

Lassiter glared at him, his hard stare traveling from the top of Chance's Resistol to the toes of his boots. "I'd rather stay in a barn than be under the same roof with a Warren."

Chance stared right back at his father-in-law. "Suit yourself. I have several barns to choose from."

Lassiter opened the car door, then slammed it shut. "On second thought, I will stay here. That way I won't have to drive back in the morning to pick up Kristen. We'll get that early start back to Dallas after all."

Chance shrugged. "Follow me."

It looked as if he'd won round one, but Chance wasn't fool enough to think the battle was over. He'd bet every penny he had that Lassiter wouldn't be going down without a hell of a fight. Well, that suited Chance just fine. This was one fight he had every intention of winning.

He waited for Lassiter to pop the car's trunk and remove an overnight case, then led the way into the house. Neither of them spoke as they climbed the stairs, and Chance showed the older man to the room farthest from the master bedroom.

"Towels are in the linen closet in the bathroom next door," Chance said as he walked out into the hall. "See you in the morning."

Closing the door behind him, Chance smiled at the muffled curse coming from the other side. He'd lay odds Lassiter wouldn't sleep a wink the entire night.

When he opened the door to his bedroom, Chance found Kristen sitting in the dark, the unopened shopping bags on the bed beside her. The shaft of moonlight coming through the parted curtains bathed her in an ethereal glow. She looked like an angel come to earth when she glanced up and smiled at him.

"Are you all right, sweetheart?"

"I can't believe I did that." She met his gaze, and he could see the amazement in her expressive green eyes. "This is the first time in my life I've ever had the courage to defy Mike."

Chance moved the bags to the chair across the room, sat down beside her on the bed and took her into his arms. "I know it must have been hard for you. But you're an adult. You have the right to do as you damn well please."

"You don't understand," she said, her voice filled with awe. "It wasn't all that difficult." She paused a moment before adding, "In fact, it felt pretty good."

He chuckled. "I wouldn't tell your dad that. I think he's had just about all the 'firsts' he can handle for one night."

"Did he say anything before he left?"

Chance nuzzled the soft hair at her temple with his cheek. God, it felt good to hold her, to inhale the sexy scent of her designer cologne. "He didn't leave."

He felt immediate tension stiffen her slender frame. "He what? Where is he?"

"He's spending the night. I put him in the bedroom at the far end of the hall."

"Why?" She sounded as if she thought he and Lassiter might both have lost their minds.

Chance slid his hands down her back, massaging the tightness gripping her. "I figured it was the least I could do."

She pulled from his arms. "I don't understand. The way he treated you was reprehensible. Why would you give him any consideration at all?"

"Because he's your dad and I'd like to work out some kind of truce. I don't want to come between the two of you." He shrugged. "Besides, my dad and your mother are both gone and I'd like for our baby to know his or her only grandparent."

"What about your mother? You never mention her."

"If my mom had wanted to know about her grandchildren, she would have stayed around to raise her kids."

"But Mike doesn't deserve—"

He placed a finger to her lips. "He's your father, Kristen."

She stared at him a moment. "I can't believe how generous you are. Mike treated you like the vilest of creatures just minutes ago. But you're willing to put all that aside just because he's my father?" Winding her arms around his neck, she smiled making him feel as if he'd been handed a rare and precious gift. "You're a very special man, Chance Warren."

He chuckled as he lowered his head to rest his forehead against hers. "Nah, I'm just a guy who's trying to keep peace in the family." He nibbled at her lips. "You married a lover, not a fighter, sweetheart."

Shivers of delight coursed through Kristen at the sound of his low drawl, the feel of his hands sliding the length of her back. When his mouth settled over hers, the contact was so tender it caused moisture to flood her eyes.

The scent of leather, the outdoors and Chance's own unique scent swirled around her. She didn't think cologne—no matter how expensive—could ever smell as sexy.

He deepened the kiss, and there was no hesitation as his tongue stroked hers. The mating was filled with promises of things to come, of a deeper, more intimate coupling. He wanted her, and she could tell he had every intention of letting her know how much.

Chance gently lowered them both to the bed, their lips never breaking contact. When he moved closer, his legs tangling with hers, the strength of his arousal pressing against her thigh had her own body responding with wanton pulses of need deep inside.

When his hand slipped beneath her shirt to caress her ribs, Kristen felt the sensations in her lower regions tighten to an unbearable ache. She wanted to feel his callused palms cupping her breasts, wanted to feel the contrast of hard masculine flesh meeting soft feminine skin.

His lips clung to hers a moment before he raised his head to gaze down at her. "I want you so damned bad I can taste it, Kristen."

"But what about—"

"I've taken care of it," he murmured, his blue gaze asking her to trust that he'd protect her.

It might not be the smartest thing she'd ever done, but she wanted Chance to make love to her. Needed it more than she'd ever needed anything in her life. Tomorrow they'd face Mike's wrath and the results of the pregnancy test she'd purchased. But tonight belonged to her and Chance. Tonight would be theirs alone.

"Make love to me, Chance," she said, hardly recognizing her own voice.

His slumberous look thrilled her to the depths of her soul. She'd never felt more feminine, more desired.

Chance rose from the bed to remove her shoes, then taking her by the hand, pulled her to her feet. "We're going to do this together," he said, bringing her hands to rest on his chest. "For each piece of clothing you take off me, I'll do the same with you."

Elated by his gesture, Kristen leaned forward and kissed the exposed skin at the top of his open shirt collar. He was allowing her to set the pace, to control how fast they approached each step in the progression of their lovemaking. Excited by the prospect of removing his clothes, she pushed him down onto the bed and bent to take off his boots. His hands caught her hips, and she felt his warm breath on her backside as he kissed her there.

"You have a nice a...rump, sweetheart," he said, his voice sounding like a rusty hinge.

She finished with his boots and socks, then turned to pull him up beside her. Sliding her hands around to squeeze his firm buttocks, she smiled when he shuddered against her. "Yours is pretty nice, too, cowboy."

"My turn," Chance said, reaching for her. He took painstaking care with each button on her mint-colored, silk blouse, and by the time he slid it down her arms, his breathing sounded rough and labored. "You have on one more piece of clothing than I do."

The look in his eyes asked for permission to remove the lace and satin covering her. When she nodded, he wasted no time reaching up to unfasten the front clasp, freeing her of the confinement. He filled both hands with her breasts, his thumbs chafing the sensitive tips to hardened peaks. "You're so beautiful. So perfect."

His head dipped to capture one of her nipples with his mouth, and Kristen clung to him. He taunted first one, then the other with his tongue before raising his head. The hungry look in his dark blue eyes made her knees tremble.

Her fingers shook slightly as she unsnapped first one gripper, then another, and opened his western shirt. The man had a gorgeous body, and she wanted once again to feel his warm, hard muscles, let her fingers trail through the light sprinkling of dark gold hair covering his chest.

By the time she pulled his shirt from his jeans and pushed it off his broad shoulders, she felt as if she'd run a marathon. Air seemed to be in extremely short supply and her heart pounded out a driving cadence.

Chance pulled her against him, and the feel of her breasts pressing against his chest, the crisp hair teasing her nipples, made her bite her lower lip in an attempt to stifle a moan.

"Let me hear you, sweetheart," he whispered against her neck. "I want to know what makes you feel good."

His warm breath on her sensitized skin, his request to hear the passion threatening to consume her made Kristen feel as if her blood had turned to warm honey. Tendrils of desire threaded their way through her limbs to pool with an aching emptiness between her thighs.

Reaching for his belt, she quickly worked the leather through the metal buckle, then popped the snap at the top of his jeans. She paused at the sight of his arousal pressing against the fly.

"That looks kind of uncomfortable," she said, swallowing her inhibitions and placing her hand against the impressively stretched denim. She traced her finger upward, her nail clicking on each metal tooth of the zipper. "You'd probably feel better if we got you out of those jeans."

"Oh, yeah." Chance closed his eyes and groaned. "Definitely better." When she reached for the tab, he placed his hands on her shoulders. "Sweetheart, when that zipper...comes down...be careful."

Easing his fly open, she pushed the jeans down his lean hips, then past his muscled thighs and calves. When he stepped out of them, she trailed her hands along his hair-roughened skin on her way back up to his briefs. She loved the way the sinew flexed and bunched at her touch. "Does that help?"

His voice was nothing but a rough whisper. "Somewhat."

Kristen took his hands in hers and guided them to her waist. "Your turn."

Chance's heated gaze held her captive as he placed his hands on her hips, then slid them around to her backside. His warm hands felt wonderful brushing against her skin as he worked the button free and opened the back closure of her linen slacks. She clutched his shoulders for support when he pushed them down her legs, then treated her to the same sweet agony of slowly skimming his hands along her legs on his way back to her silk panties. When he reached the elastic at the tops of her thighs, he splayed his hands, his thumbs coming into contact with the damp fabric between her legs. The light pressure he applied there, the chafing of his thumbs against the most sensitive spot on her body, had her feeling as if she just might melt into a puddle at his feet.

"Feel good, sweetheart?" he asked, his low drawl sending a fresh wave of heat straight to the part of her that made her woman.

Unable to form a coherent word, she simply nodded. But when he stood up and she reached for the elastic band of his briefs, he stopped her. Placing his hands at the top of her panties, he whispered, "Let's take this last step together."

His gaze captured hers and together they disposed of the last barriers separating them.

Kristen's eyes widened at the sight of his magnificent body. She'd been too embarrassed this afternoon to notice, and her memory of him stretched across the bed in the hotel room in Las Vegas hadn't done the man justice. If not for the long white scar marring his left side, Chance could have been a Greek god come to earth. He was just that perfect.

His wide shoulders, chest and thighs were well defined by muscles made hard from years of physical labor, his flanks lean. Her breath caught at the sight of his proud, full erection. He was impressively built, thoroughly aroused and looking at her as if she were the only woman on earth.

His voice thickened by passion, he guided her to him. "Don't be afraid to touch me, Kristen. I won't ever hurt you."

She shivered with hot, hungry desire when she circled him with her hand, her fingers not quite meeting her thumb. His warm, thick strength surged at her touch and he groaned like a man in pain.

"Mmm. Yeah, that's it, sweetheart," he said, his eyes closing as she explored his length and the softness below. "That feels good."

Cupping her breasts, he lowered his head to circle each nipple in turn with his tongue, to nibble at them with his lips. Swirls of heat coursed through her, and moaning, she abandoned her exploration to grab his forearms for support.

When he raised his head, he smiled and swung her up into his arms. ''I think we'd better move this to the bed while we can still walk.''

Chance gently placed Kristen on the bed, then, rummaging through the pockets of his jeans, he retrieved the small box of foil packets he'd purchased while they were in Amarillo. Placing their protection within easy reach, he joined her, stretching out to pull her to him.

The feel of her soft, feminine skin just about sent him over the edge. His body urged him to bury himself deep inside her, to take the final step toward making them one. But he gritted his teeth and ignored it. Kristen had no recollection of their wedding night—the night she'd given him her virginity—and this afternoon hadn't turned out to be one of his finer performances as a lover. But tonight Chance was determined to make things right. He fully intended for this to be the most memorable night of her life.

He slid his hand along her side to the smooth roundness of her hip, then down to her knee. ''You have the softest skin.'' Slowly running his palm up along the inner part of her thigh, he smiled when she shivered against him. ''Feel good?''

''Yes,'' she said, sounding breathless.

Chance stopped just below his goal to prop himself up on one elbow and gaze down into her flushed face. ''You want more, sweetheart?''

''Yes.''

''Are you sure?''

Apparently incapable of speech, she nodded, her eyes telling him what she couldn't voice.

Lowering his lips to hers, Chance kissed her deeply as

he brought his fingers into contact with her damp auburn curls. He parted her to stroke the sensitive feminine bud, and her lower body rose to meet his hand.

She grasped his shoulders, her nails biting into his skin. "Chance, please!"

"Not yet, sweetheart." He dipped one finger lower to enter her as he continued to stroke her to a frenzied passion. "I want you to remember this as our first night together."

She gasped and tightened her grip on him. "But—"

He shook his head. "What took place in Vegas doesn't count. Neither one of us remembers a whole lot about it." He kissed her elegant neck, the hollow behind her ear. "And this afternoon never happened. Tonight you're a virgin again and it's our first time together." He kissed her flushed cheek. "Tonight I'll take your virginity and make you mine, Kristen."

The look she gave him nearly sent his good intentions to go slow right out the window. "Then do it," she demanded. "You're driving me crazy."

His chuckle turned to a low, deep groan when she reached down to take hold of him. Her soft hands caressed, stroked and teased him to painful need. His wife might not be experienced at lovemaking, but she definitely knew what she wanted. And she wanted it *now*. But then, so did he.

"Just a minute, sweetheart."

Chance's hands shook as he grabbed the box of condoms, tore it open and removed one foil packet. He rolled the latex over his pulsing erection, then pulled the pillows together and lifted Kristen up to lie back against them. He knelt between her legs, placed his hands on her hips to lift her to him and slowly, carefully, pressed himself forward and into her damp heat. The passion in her eyes increased as his entry stretched her to accommodate him, and with each passing second, his restraint became more difficult to maintain. Every cell in his body demanded that he surge forward and fill her with everything he had, but he forced himself to hold back. He needed to give Kristen time to adjust to his size and the newness of lovemaking.

When she winced, her body trying to resist the invasion of his, he held himself completely still. She was so damned hot, so tight. A sudden thought made him close his eyes and reach down for every bit of strength he possessed, in order to go slow. He didn't want to hurt her. He was afraid he might have this afternoon when he'd been so hungry for her that he'd acted like a teenage boy experimenting with his first girl in the back seat of his daddy's Buick. He'd die before he let that happen again.

Brushing her damp bangs from her forehead, he hardly recognized his own hoarse whisper. "Take a deep breath and relax, sweetheart. You were made to hold me like this."

Careful to keep his lower body still, Chance kissed her with every tender feeling he had but couldn't put a name to. Rewarded by her sigh of acceptance, he moved deeper into her. But her need to have all of him must have become more than she could handle. Suddenly, and without warning, Kristen wrapped her long, slender legs around him and pulled him forward, demanding that he fill her completely.

A groan rumbled from deep in his chest as Chance, taken by surprise, gave into Kristen's demand and buried himself to the hilt in her soft heat. The blood rushing through his veins roared in his ears, and the white-hot haze of desire blinded him to anything but his need to complete the act of loving her.

"I wish you hadn't done that."

"Why?" she asked, her throaty whisper sending a surge of heat straight to his loins. The involuntary movement of his body inside hers caused her eyes to widen. "Did you do that?"

Despite his need, Chance laughed. "Sweetheart, you've got a whole lot to learn about a man and the way his body works."

"Then teach me."

Her heavy-lidded gaze, her legs tightening around him, urging him even deeper, made Chance lose the slender thread of his control. He slowly withdrew, then surged forward, setting the pace for what he knew would be the most meaningful moment of his life.

Kristen quickly met and matched him in the dance, her body building to the moment when they would no longer be two people, but one—one body, one soul in a world of mind-shattering sensation. He strengthened his thrusts and felt her inner muscles strain to hold him captive, then quiver around him as she gave in to the storm. She moaned his name, and her nails bit into his skin with a fierceness that thrilled him.

Feeling her climax sweep him into his own explosion, Chance shouted her name, his body stiffening to an unbearable degree before he ground his hips into hers one last time. Wave after wave coursed through him as he held her close—her body a lifeline to reality.

Several long moments passed before he managed to lever his weight from her. "Are you okay, sweetheart? I didn't hurt, you did I?"

"No."

Chance felt a moment of fear. "No, you're not all right? Or no, I didn't hurt you?"

Kristen stretched her arms, then caught his face in her hands, her smile warming him all the way to his soul. "Silly man. No, you didn't hurt me." She kissed him. "That was the most incredible experience of my life. Like magic."

Rolling to her side, he pulled her on top of him. "Mine, too, sweetheart." He chuckled. "I do believe I've died and gone to heaven."

"Mmm. Me, too."

She lowered her head to press tiny kisses along his collarbone and down his chest. When she reached his flat nipple her tongue darted out to lick his puckered flesh, and Chance felt himself getting hard all over again.

"Is it always like that?" she asked, her sweet lips nipping at him.

"Nope."

"It's not?" She sounded disappointed.

Pulling her up so their gazes met, he shook his head. "Only if it's the right man with the right woman, and they're meant to be together. That's when it's magic."

Kristen threaded her fingers through his hair. "Did you mean it?"

"What?"

"You said I had a lot to learn about a man's body." She used her tongue to trace his lips. "Did you mean it?"

"Yep."

"And you're going to teach me?"

Groaning, he rolled them over to pin her to the mattress. "Oh, yeah."

"When?"

He pressed his erection to her thigh and watched a heated hunger light her eyes. "Right now."

"Then let's make a little magic, cowboy."

Nine

Kristen woke to the sounds of the shower running and Chance's rich baritone belting out a popular country love song. He would never make it in the entertainment industry, but his other talents more than made up for his lack of singing ability. Her stomach tightened at the thought of how he'd used those hidden talents to play her body like a fine violin, to make her soul sing with the beauty of his lovemaking. She smiled at the memory and stretched, the crisp sheets feeling absolutely wonderful on her nude body.

Throwing back the covers, she got out of bed, intent on joining him in the shower. But the sight of the shopping bags from their trip to Amarillo stopped her. She was a day late and had intended to use the in-home test this morning—to put an end to the speculation of whether or not she was pregnant.

She glanced at the closed bathroom door, then back to

the pile of packages. If the results came back negative, would Chance still be convinced they should stay together? He'd said as much, but was that the way he really felt? Or was it due to his misguided belief that they'd been drawn together by fate to create a baby? Kristen really didn't think he'd considered the possibility that she wasn't pregnant.

His voice strained to reach a high note and she smiled, her decision made. Putting on her silk robe, she tucked the pregnancy test in the pocket and hurried down the hall to one of the guest bathrooms. Her hands trembled as she followed the directions, then waited for the verdict. Within a matter of minutes, Kristen watched two blue lines appear in the tiny results window.

"My God, he's right," she murmured, placing her splayed hands across her flat stomach. "I'm pregnant."

A myriad of emotions ran through her. Wonder at the idea of having a life growing inside of her, concern that everything would be all right, and determination to be a much better parent to her child than Mike had been to his. But all that paled in comparison to the sheer joy she felt at the knowledge she was pregnant with Chance's baby.

Stunned by the intensity of the feeling, she walked back to the bedroom, slipped her robe off and entered the master bath. Opening the frosted shower door, she stepped inside. "Good morning, cowboy."

Chance's surprised expression quickly turned to a grin that made her insides quiver. "Imagine meeting you here, Mrs. Warren." He pulled her into his arms. "How are you this morning?"

Kristen twined her arms around his neck and pressed herself to his slick, wet body. She'd tell Chance about the baby, but not now. For the moment she wanted to get lost in the feel of his tightening muscles, the sight of instant hunger in his brilliant blue eyes. "I could be better."

"Oh, really." He ran his hands over her wet bottom, his palms cupping her to draw her closer. "Is there anything I can do to help?"

She drew back and shook her head. "No." She used her finger to follow a rivulet coursing down his chest. "This is something I need to do all on my own."

When she followed the trail of water with her lips as it ran over his belly, he groaned. "And what is it you need to do, sweetheart?"

"You'll see."

She sipped the droplet of water from his navel. With the tip of her finger she traced the line of hair arrowing down from the indention to his full, heavy arousal.

"Would you look at that?" Glancing up at him from beneath her lashes, she grinned. "You seem to have a problem."

The look he gave her sent shivers of anticipation running from every part of her straight to her most sensitive point. "Why yes, Mrs. Warren, I believe I do."

She circled him with her hand. "Want help?"

Moving her fingers along the length of him, she watched him close his eyes and throw back his head. "Do you have any idea what you're doing, woman?"

"Oh, yes."

He groaned from deep in his chest. "And just what would that be?"

"My homework."

"Your what?" He shuddered and opened his eyes, the feral light in the dark depths sending heat waves coursing throughout her body.

"I had class just last night," she said, giving him a

sensuous smile. "And I had a *very* good teacher." He reached for her, but Kristen stepped back and shook her head. "Uh-uh. You're just a spectator in this rodeo."

As she knelt in front of him, the shower's spray drenched her hair and ran down her face, but it felt highly sensual as she leaned forward to kiss him intimately.

"Kristen—"

"Just lean back and enjoy."

His hands came up as if to push her away, but when she deepened the caress, he surrendered and held her to him.

"Cowboy up," she heard him growl as he braced his shoulders against the tiled wall and allowed her to practice what he'd taught her the night before.

His arm around Kristen's shoulders, Chance felt as if he'd died and gone to heaven as they walked downstairs. She was the most passionate, giving woman he'd ever been with.

"I'm the king of the world," he said suddenly, causing her to laugh.

But her laughter faded and her shoulders tensed beneath his arm at the sight of her father already waiting for them in the kitchen. Lassiter sat at the table, a cup of coffee in front of him.

"Good morning, Mr. Lassiter. Glad to see you've made yourself at home," Chance said, walking over to remove a cup from the cabinet above the coffeemaker.

Lassiter didn't bother with exchanging pleasantries. "I got tired of waiting, so I made coffee." He removed a videotape from his briefcase and shoved it across the table. "Here's your damned video, Warren."

An uneasy silence followed his announcement.

Chance noticed Kristen's wary expression, the twisting

of her hands, her body poised as if waiting for an explosion. He ran the back of his hand along her cheek and gave her a look he hoped was encouraging. "Do you want me to make breakfast this morning, sweetheart?"

"No, I'll do it," she said, sounding a little unsure. "How do scrambled eggs and toast sound?"

"Just fine," Chance said, kissing her forehead.

"Get away from her, Warren."

Chance ignored his father-in-law and touched his index finger to Kristen's trembling lips. The confident woman he'd made love to all through the night, and who'd loved him with total abandon this morning, had disappeared. It tore Chance apart to see the uncertain, apprehensive girl she'd turned into at the sight of her father.

"It's going to be all right, Kristen," he whispered. "As long as I have breath in my body, you don't have to be afraid of him."

She smiled and mouthed a "thank you," then turned to start breakfast.

Chance took a deep breath and reminded himself to calm down before he joined his father-in-law at the table. He tried, but failed to keep the hard edge from his voice when he asked, "Did you sleep well, Mr. Lassiter?"

"Cut the small talk, Warren." Lassiter glared at him, and Chance figured it reflected the look on his own face. "How much do you want? How much is it going to cost me to get Kristen out of this farce?"

Kristen gasped and dropped the egg she held. "Mike!"

"Go to hell," Chance snarled, rising from his chair. He took her into his arms. Her body trembled and he could tell she was about two seconds away from falling completely to pieces.

Lassiter whipped a checkbook from his shirt pocket, then clicked a pen into readiness. "Come on, I'm a busy man. I need to get this wrapped up so Kristen and I can get back to Dallas and start annulment proceedings. Name your price, Warren."

Chance had never wanted to punch a man so badly as he did at that moment. Nothing would feel better than putting his doubled fist in the middle of Lassiter's nose. But he held himself in check. Bastard or not, the man was still Kristen's father.

Chance counted to twenty before he had himself back in control. "I don't want one damned penny of your money, Lassiter. Now get your ass back to Dallas before I kick it there."

"You aren't man enough. You married my daughter for a reason, and my guess is money. Or Sagebrush Boots. But if you think you can get your hands on my company, you're dead wrong. Kristen will never have control as long as she's married to you."

"I don't want your damned company." In truth, Chance was glad to hear Kristen would never take charge of Sagebrush Boots. "I'm not a city boy, Lassiter, and I never want to be one. I've worked too long and hard to build the Sundance into what it is, and I have no intention of leaving it."

"Go pack," Lassiter ordered Kristen. "He's not worth wasting our time on."

"No," she said, her voice quiet but firm. Chance felt her straighten her shoulders a moment before she pulled from his arms to face her father. "I'm not going back to Dallas with you, Mike. I used an in-home test this morning. I'm pregnant and I'm staying right here until Chance and I talk things over."

Chance felt as if he'd just won the lottery. He'd hoped

and prayed for this moment since that late-night walk through the streets of Gallup, New Mexico.

Swinging her up into his arms, he gave her a quick, hard kiss. "Hot damn, sweetheart! We're gonna have a baby."

Lassiter slammed his checkbook and pen on the table. "The hell you are," he shouted, starting forward, his face a mottled red. "Kristen, get over here."

Chance set Kristen on her feet and stepped in front of her. "Back off, Lassiter. Nobody talks to Kristen in that tone of voice. Not even you."

"She's my daughter."

His hands flexing into fists, Chance glared at his father-in-law. "She's my wife and you'll damned well start treating her with respect or we'll take this outside and settle things once and for all."

The back door suddenly burst open and crashed against the wall. "Mike Lassiter, you ornery son of a sidewinder, I could hear you shoutin' all the way out on the porch. Leave these kids alone," Sarah commanded, her eyes sparkling with a fury Chance had never seen. "They got married because it was meant to be, and you're just gonna have to learn to live with it."

Lassiter stopped dead in his tracks to stare open-mouthed. "Sarah?"

"That's right, Mike." Sarah's glare was cold enough to frost glass. "It's been over thirty-five years and I see you're still the same old bag of wind you always were."

"You know Mike?" Kristen asked.

"Honey, I've known your daddy since he was nothin' but a dust-covered cowboy with empty pockets and a head full of pipe dreams." Sarah turned to Chance. "Now, you two go on upstairs and enjoy your good news and start makin' your plans." She looked back at a red-faced Mike. "This old man and I have a few scores to settle."

Chance didn't have to be told twice. He figured if he didn't leave the room, he'd end up taking Lassiter apart one limb at a time, and enjoying the experience immensely. Placing his hand on Kristen's back, he ushered her toward the stairs.

"Do you think it's all right to leave her alone with him?" she asked as they entered their bedroom.

Chance laughed out loud. "Sweetheart, let's put it this way. It won't be pretty and I don't envy your dad one damned bit. If it was me down there facing the wrath of Sarah Carpenter, I'd run like hell and not look back."

"Mike can be—"

"Sarah can hold her own," Chance interrupted. "But I don't want to talk about them right now." He pulled her against him, then lifted the tail of her shirt to place his hands on her smooth, flat stomach. "I want to talk about that little bomb you dropped down there in the kitchen."

"Oh, that."

"Yeah, that." He nuzzled the hair at her temple with his lips. "When did you buy that test?"

"Probably the same time you bought the condoms," she said, sounding breathless.

He chuckled. "And here I thought you were looking at shoes."

"Well, I thought you were looking at camera equipment."

They remained silent for several long moments before he asked, "When did you use the test?"

"This morning before I joined you in the shower."

"Why didn't you tell me then, sweetheart?"

Turning to face him, she wrapped her arms around his

waist. ''I had to get used to the idea myself before I could tell anyone.'' She gazed up at him. ''Does that make sense?''

Chance nodded. ''In the last few days you've had a lot to come to grips with. Did you mean it when you told your dad you're staying?'' He brushed her lips with his.

She shivered against him and he felt his lower body tighten in answer. Pulling his shirttail from his jeans, she ran her hands along his spine, then down. When her fingers slid beneath the waistband of his jeans, he groaned.

''What?'' she asked, kissing the skin exposed at his open shirt collar.

Between her lips nuzzling his neck and her talented little hands exploring his backside, she expected him to remember what he'd asked? He placed his palms on her delightful bottom and pressed his erection to her feminine heat. ''It doesn't matter right now.''

She gazed up at him and smiled. ''I really appreciate the way you stood up to Mike this morning.''

''Sweetheart, that's what a husband is supposed to do,'' he said, unfastening her bra. ''It's part of the job description.''

''Is that all?''

''Nope.''

She tilted her head to the side and looked thoughtful, at the same time bringing her hands around to unbuckle his belt. ''What else are you supposed to do?''

''Make love to you until we both collapse with pleasure.''

''Good answer.'' The look she gave him sent his blood pressure soaring. ''Cowboy, you're about to get so-o-o-o lucky.''

* * *

Late that afternoon, Kristen glanced out the window and watched Sarah and Mike walk toward one of the barns. She couldn't quite believe it, but with the arrival of Sarah this morning, there had been a definite change in Mike. He didn't seem nearly as anxious to get back to Dallas. And he had calmed down considerably.

Leaning against the high back of the leather desk chair, Kristen turned her attention back to the computer screen. She'd installed the new programs they'd purchased last night and set up most of Chance's accounts. She had a few suggestions where she thought he might diversify and expand, but he'd done quite well for himself in the last five years. In fact, if Mike knew how much Chance was worth, he'd be humiliated at even suggesting that Chance had married her for money. Financially, the Sundance Rodeo Company was on rock-solid ground and showing steady growth.

She smiled. She loved how Chance allowed her to use the skills she'd learned in college. Encouraged her, even. It was something her own father had never done for her.

Mike had always viewed her education as something she'd done to kill time after finishing high school. He hadn't even considered that she'd graduated at the top of her class, or that one day, as his only child, she'd hold controlling interest in Sagebrush Boots. No, Mike wanted her to marry Spencer Dirkson, thus providing him with a *man* to run the company after his retirement. He'd even told Chance that she'd never control the company.

She shook her head. Funny how her priorities had changed with the appearance of those tiny blue lines on a test stick. She no longer cared whether she ran Sagebrush Boots or not. She laid a protective hand on her stomach. All that mattered now was the welfare of her baby.

Unlike her own childhood, she wanted more than anything for her baby to know the love of both parents. And to know that his or her parents loved each other.

Kristen smiled. She really didn't think she'd have to worry about the first part of that wish. Chance had made it clear from the beginning he wanted the baby and intended to help raise it. But what about the last part?

Sadness filled her and tears burned her eyes. Her mother had loved Mike, but if he'd ever felt anything more than deep respect and fondness for Martina Harrington-Lassiter, he'd never shown it. Even as a young girl, Kristen had recognized her mother's unrequited love, her sadness that Mike didn't return her feelings. Sometimes Kristen wondered if that hadn't contributed to Martina's failing health and untimely death. Even her mother's last request had been for Kristen to settle for nothing less than love in her life.

And that's when it hit her. She did love Chance.

Kristen felt the emotion spread throughout her soul as she began to acknowledge it. Even though they'd married under less-than-ideal conditions, and despite Mike's adamant disapproval, somewhere along the line she'd fallen in love with her husband. But could he care for her in return? He'd said he wanted to stay married because of the baby, but what about her? Could he learn to love her as well?

Chance stood behind Kristen, watching her key in several entries for his business records. She made it look like the easiest thing in the world to input all those facts and figures.

"You're amazing, you know that?" He pulled her out of the chair for his kiss. "So smart." He brushed her lips again. "So beautiful." He rested his forehead against hers. "So damned sexy."

Her throaty laughter sent his pulse into overdrive. "So which do you find more sexy? My mind or my looks?"

He shook his head. "Oh, no, sweetheart. I'm not falling into that trap. If I say your mind, you'll ask what's wrong with your looks. And if I say your looks, you'll ask me what's wrong with your mind." He grinned. "Let's just say I like the whole package."

"I like your package, too, cowboy."

Chance groaned when she pressed her body full against his. "I was supposed to come in here and tell you that Sarah has supper ready."

Her answering smile caused an immediate and intense reaction in the region below his belt. "Well, I am pretty hungry," she whispered.

"I think I've created a monster," Chance said, chuckling. He swallowed hard, then set her away from him. "You'd better sit down and finish what you were doing."

She laughed. "But I thought you said Sarah has supper ready."

"She does."

"Then let's go eat."

"I can't."

"Why not?"

"Because you've got me hard as hell," he growled. When she glanced down at the front of his jeans, it didn't help matters one damned bit. "Kristen…"

Her knowing grin didn't help, either. "Why don't I go see if Sarah needs help?"

"Yeah, why don't you?" He closed his eyes and tried to concentrate on something less appealing than his delightful wife. "I'll join you in a few minutes."

"Okay," she said, kissing his cheek as she stepped around him to leave. "Don't be too long."

Chance didn't open his eyes until he heard Kristen start down the hall. He had enough adrenaline pumping through his veins, he could probably bench-press a dump truck. Mentally doing just that, he finally felt in control enough to venture into the kitchen.

The look of veiled hostility Mike Lassiter gave him when Chance walked to the table and sat down took care of any lasting traces of arousal he might have left. The man had spent the afternoon catching up on old times with Sarah, and although his attitude had improved and he wasn't as openly hostile, Chance suspected their confrontation wasn't over. They still had unfinished business.

"Chance, Mike has decided to stay on with us until after the Halloween party Saturday night," Sarah said as she seated herself at the round oak table.

Chance eyed his father-in-law. "Is that right?"

Lassiter shrugged. "Sarah talked me into it." His brow furrowed. "It's not because I want to spend more time getting to know you. So don't get any ideas about gaining my approval."

"It would be nice for Kristen's sake, but as far as I'm concerned, I don't give a damn one way or the other." Chance rubbed his side where Kristen tried to separate his ribs with her elbow, then reached over to take her hand in his. "Your daughter's approval is all I need."

When Lassiter looked as if he intended to say more, Chance noticed Sarah's warning glare. Lassiter cleared his throat before he finally said, "We'll discuss this later, Warren."

"I'm counting on it," Chance shot back.

An uneasy silence followed for several long minutes

before Sarah asked Kristen, ''What are you plannin' on wearin' to the party?''

''I really hadn't thought about it,'' Kristen answered, her expression showing the strain of being around her father. Chance hated that the man affected her that way.

''Well, I have a couple of ideas, and if you'd like, we can make a trip into Amarillo tomorrow afternoon to pick up what we need,'' Sarah offered.

''Yes, I'd like that.'' Turning to Lassiter, Kristen asked, ''Mike, are you going in costume?''

Chance raised a brow when he noticed a flicker of pain cross the man's face at Kristen's use of his name. It wasn't a reaction he'd have associated with Lassiter.

''Sarah wants me to,'' Mike answered.

Sarah nodded, her grin smug as she passed around a platter piled high with country-fried steaks. ''Yep. I've been thinkin' that we oughta go as Mickey and Minnie Mouse.''

In the process of swallowing a drink of iced tea, Chance choked at the pained look on Lassiter's face. The man's cheeks were beet red, and he seemed to take great interest in choosing a steak as he grudgingly nodded his agreement.

Kristen thumped Chance on the back several times before he caught his breath. ''Are you all right?''

''Uh…yeah.'' From Lassiter's glare, Chance figured the man would have been just as happy if Chance choked to death. Unable to stop himself, he grinned at his father-in-law. ''I'll have to remember to take my camera.''

Lassiter's irritated growl was cut short when Sarah shuffled her feet under the table. ''Ouch.'' He reached down to rub his shin, but his warning scowl didn't waiver from Chance. ''Remind me, when you and I have that discussion later, to cover your smart attitude as well.''

"Sure thing, Mr. Lassiter. I have a few things to talk over with you, too." Chance cut into his steak and took a bite. But for all he tasted of the prime beef it might as well have been a piece of boot leather. "How does the study sound, in about an hour?"

Lassiter nodded. "The sooner the bet—"

"Not tonight, Mike," Sarah interrupted. "We've got a date, remember?"

This time, it was Chance's turn to pound on Kristen's back.

Ten

"**T**ime to wake up, sweetheart."

Kristen groaned. "Go away."

"Not until you eat." The side of the bed dipped as Chance sat down beside her.

"I've told you before, I don't eat breakfast," she said, opening her eyes to glare at him.

"Come on. You need to…eat." Chance didn't look well at all.

Alarmed by his unhealthy pallor and the strained look around his eyes and mouth, she sat up. "Chance, are you all right?"

He nodded but couldn't seem to speak.

Taking the beer tray with the plateful of food from him, she placed it on the bedside table. "No, you're not."

"Yes, I am." He took a deep breath and slowly let it out. "See. I'm fine. Now, eat your breakfast. Please."

Kristen wasn't convinced, but she took the beer tray onto her lap and poked the food on her plate with the fork. She really wasn't hungry, but Chance did have a point about eating properly now that she was pregnant.

She took a deep breath and savored the smell of the crisp bacon. "This does smell good." Picking up a strip, she nibbled on it, then held it out for Chance to take a bite. "Want to try some?"

"N-n-no." His complexion went from chalky white to a sickly green.

"Chance?"

Kristen put the tray back on the night table just as he shot up from the bed and bolted for the bathroom. Following him, she watched him sink to his knees and hug the bowl.

Running cool water over a washcloth, she bathed the cold sweat from his flushed cheeks and forehead. "Poor baby. Let's get you back to the bed."

He remained on his knees, but lowering the lid, he crossed his arms on top of it and rested his head on his forearm. "Go away...and let...me die."

She bit the inside of her cheek to stop her smile. "You're not going to die."

"Yes...I am."

"No, you're not. Something must not have agreed with you. Did you have bacon and eggs for breakfast?" If so, she sure wasn't eating hers.

"Please...don't mention—" Groaning, he raised the lid again and hugged the bowl.

Kristen handed him the washcloth. "Stay right here, darling. Don't try to get up. I'm going to get Mike to help me get you to bed."

"Oh, God...no! Don't do...that."

"Nonsense. You're too sick to make it to bed on your own and I'm not strong enough to be of much help."

She hurried from the bathroom before he had an opportunity to argue the point any further. Grabbing her robe, she pulled it on as she ran down the hall for the stairs. "Mike! Get up here."

By the time she reached the top step, Mike and Sarah were on their way up to see what all the commotion was about.

"What the hell's going on?" Mike demanded. "Did he hurt you? If he so much as looked cross-eyed at you, I swear I'll kill him."

Kristen stared in surprise at the look of concern on Mike's face. But she didn't have time to dwell on it. Chance needed help. "No, Mike, I'm fine." Without waiting for the pair to follow, Kristen headed back toward the bedroom. "It's Chance. He's deathly sick and I need help getting him to bed."

"Mike, you go ahead and help Kristen," Sarah said, turning to go back downstairs. "I have a fair idea what's ailin' that boy. I'll be up in a minute with somethin' that should settle his stomach."

When Kristen and Mike reached the bathroom, Chance had managed to drag himself up from the floor to sit on the side of the bathtub. His color was a little better, but he still looked as if he might collapse at any minute.

"Aw, hell, Kristen. Why did you have to go get *him?*"

Mike bent down to place Chance's arm across his shoulders, then hoisted him to his feet. "Boy, you look like something pulled you through a knothole backward." Mike chuckled. "I just wish I'd been there to see it."

"You're really enjoying this, aren't you, Lassiter," Chance muttered.

Mike nodded as he walked Chance into the bedroom. "Sure am."

"You poisoned me, didn't you," Chance accused when Mike lowered him to the side of the bed.

"No." Mike stood back and grinned. "But only because I didn't think of it."

Kristen was surprised at the conversation between the two. Mike wasn't being as antagonistic as he was teasing. But still, Chance didn't feel well and baiting him wasn't fair. Propping her fists on her hips, she gave them both a look she hoped would end the banter before it escalated. "Both of you stop it, right now." She helped Chance lie back against the pillows. "Neither one of you means what you're saying."

"Maybe he doesn't—"

"He probably put something in my food—"

"Mike. Chance," Kristen warned.

"Are these two at it again?" Sarah walked into the room carrying a cup and a handful of crackers. Handing them to Kristen, she grinned. "Get that weak tea and crackers down him. It should settle his stomach."

"I think I've been poisoned," Chance said, closing his eyes. "Just leave me alone and let me die in peace."

Sarah laughed. "You ain't dyin'."

"I feel like it."

Lassiter actually laughed out loud. "He looks like it, too."

Chance opened his eyes to glare at his father-in-law. "I hope I'm contagious and you get whatever this is."

"Chance," Kristen warned.

"Kristen might get it, but it's not likely that Mike or I will." Sarah laughed. "I watched your daddy go through the same thing when your mama was carryin' you."

"What is it?" Chance asked, sure it was nothing short of a miracle his father had survived.

"You've got mornin' sickness."

Kristen looked doubtful. "He's got what?"

"That's ridiculous," Chance said, groaning. "Women get morning sickness. Men don't."

Sarah nodded. "Some do. Check those books you bought. I'm sure they have somethin' about it. It's like sympathy pains. Some men get those when their wives go into labor. If you're like your daddy was about your mama, you'll have those from the time Kristen goes into labor until she has the baby."

"It would serve him right," Lassiter said, scowling. "If my daughter has to be in pain, then he should, too."

Chance groaned when his stomach churned at the thought of Kristen experiencing labor pains.

"Mike, you're not helping," Kristen said. She held the mug to Chance's mouth. "Drink this."

"I don't like hot tea. Just let me die. I'll feel a hell of a lot better when I do."

"I said drink it," Kristen ordered.

He glanced up at her. The determined look in her beautiful green eyes was enough to convince him to take a sip. Besides, there wasn't much use in protesting. He'd do anything she asked of him. "Ugh. That's awful."

"Come on, Mike," Sarah said, taking him by the arm. "Kristen can take care of things from here."

"But I was enjoying—"

"I can see you and me have some more talkin' to do about your attitude," Sarah said, tugging him toward the door.

Chance chuckled and opened his mouth to comment on his father-in-law's pained expression, but the cracker

Kristen stuffed into his mouth cut short anything he'd been about to say.

Kristen switched on the truck lights. Dusk was quickly turning into the dark of night as she steered the truck onto the road leading south out of Amarillo. "I really enjoyed myself, Sarah. I'm glad you suggested we spend the day shopping and looking for costumes, but I'm not sure Chance is going to like what we decided on. He just doesn't seem the Donald Duck type to me."

She wished Chance had gone with her and Sarah into Amarillo to help choose the costumes. That way she'd be sure he didn't mind what she'd picked out. But after recovering from his bout of morning sickness, Chance had used the excuse that he'd promised Cody and Annie he'd go over for a visit. Even Mike, who hadn't left Sarah's side since his arrival, said he'd rather run buck-naked through a briar patch than go shopping, and decided to remain at the Sundance to make a few business calls.

"Oh, don't worry. Chance will grumble and complain about it, just like Mike did about the Mickey Mouse costume," Sarah said, laughing. "But, mark my words, he'll wear that suit if you tell him to."

Kristen wasn't so sure. "Asking Chance to wear feathers and a pair of tights might be pushing it a bit."

"Honey, ain't you figured out by now that you've got that boy wrapped around your little finger? As long as you ask him to do somethin', he'll do it or die tryin'." She patted Kristen's arm. "He loves you too much not to. This morning when he got sick as a dog is proof enough of that. Men don't get sympathetic morning sickness unless they're so crazy in love they don't know which end is up."

Kristen wished what Sarah said was true. But she wasn't convinced. Chance wanted their baby and thought they should stay married to raise the child, but that didn't mean he loved her. He'd talked about fate bringing them together and how thrilled he was over her pregnancy, but not once had he mentioned love. Not now, or even the possibility of it in the future.

Could she settle on the type of relationship her mother had with Mike? Would his wanting them to stay together because of their child be enough for her? Kristen didn't think so.

When she steered the truck into the yard and the headlights illuminated the side of the house, Kristen was surprised to see Mike and Chance standing on the porch together. They weren't at each other's throats, but with their backs to each other and their arms folded across their chests, their body language didn't indicate they were being friendly, either.

As soon as she and Sarah got out of the truck, the two men came down the steps to meet them.

"I missed you," Chance said, taking her into his arms. His warm breath sent shivers of excitement down her spine as he placed a kiss along the column of her throat.

"What did you two pick out for Warren to wear to the costume party?" Mike asked, dropping his arm across Sarah's shoulders.

Kristen's brow rose. It was the first time in her life she ever remembered seeing her father display affection for anyone. "Uh, it's a surprise."

Chance groaned. "I don't like the sound of that."

Mike looked way too happy in the face of Chance's apprehension. "I don't care what it is, if my daughter says she wants you to wear it, you'd damned well better do it."

"Mike—"

He looked at Chance, the meaning in his gray gaze crystal clear. "I'm giving you fair warning, Warren. I'm holding you personally responsible for the welfare of my daughter and grandchild. Whatever it is they want from you, you'd better deliver it or die trying. And that includes dressing yourself up in whatever costume Kristen picked out. No matter how outlandish."

Kristen gasped, but her protest was cut short when Chance put his arm around her shoulders and pulled her to his side. "You don't have to worry, Mr. Lassiter. I've got it covered."

Mike stared a moment longer, then nodded. "Just so we have that straight."

"Come on, you old windbag." Sarah urged him toward the porch. "You're doin' better, but we're still gonna have another talk about your attitude."

When Sarah managed to get Mike into the house, Kristen turned to Chance. "I'm sorry. He had no right to talk to you like that."

Chance pushed his hat back with one thumb, then pulled her to him. Resting his forehead against hers, he smiled. "He's trying to deal with the fact that I'm the man who's taken you away from him."

Kristen wasn't convinced. "He's never bothered acting like a father before."

"Sweetheart, don't be so hard on him. He's just doing and saying what I would in the same position." Kissing the tip of her nose, Chance smiled down at her. "You can bet I'll be the most unreasonable man in the Panhandle when our little girl drags some guy home and tells us that I'm being replaced as the number one man in her life."

"But—"

He placed his finger to her lips. "Believe me, Kristen. Your dad may not show it, but I've seen the way he looks at you. He does love you."

She shrugged. "If you say so."

Chance hugged her close, then stepped back and turned toward the truck. "Come on, Mrs. Warren. Let's get these boxes unloaded and into the house. Then you can tell me what godawful costume you and Sarah came up with for me to wear to the party tomorrow night."

Kristen felt her spirits lift. "Sarah says you'll love it."

He laughed. "Yeah, and I saw a cow fly over the house just this morning."

"You've got to be kidding," Chance said, frowning at the white-feathered get-up. He wished he'd paid more attention last night when Kristen tried to tell him about the costumes. He'd had more pleasurable things in mind, and after making love they'd fallen asleep without talking about the party. "I'm going to look like a—"

"Donald Duck." Kristen handed him a pair of yellow tights. "Now, put these on. We only have ten minutes to finish getting ready. I told Beth we'd be there a little early to help her set up the refreshments."

Chance groaned. "Steve will never let me live this down."

"Don't worry about it," she said, laughing. "Just wait until you see what he's wearing."

"It had better be worse than this." Chance pulled the offensive yellow tights up to his knees. "I don't know how you women wear panty hose. These things are going to make the hair on my legs itch like hell."

"Well, I suppose you could always—"

"No way." He scowled at her amused expression and shook his head. "I'm not shaving my legs."

''Then don't complain about the itching,'' she said, waddling her cute little feathered bottom to the door. ''I'll meet you downstairs. I'm going to see if Mike and Sarah are ready.''

Chance grinned as he tugged the tights up over his thighs. ''The only thing that keeps me from staying home is wanting to see your dad parade around in front of everyone in a Mickey Mouse costume.''

She laughed as she adjusted the bright pink bow on her Daisy Duck head. ''I don't think I'll tell him you said that.''

''Probably wouldn't be a good idea.''

When she closed the door behind her, Chance pulled a black T-shirt from his drawer and put it on as he eyed the white pile of feathers lying on the bed. If someone had told him a week ago that he'd be dressing up in anything other than his usual rodeo cowboy outfit for the annual Halloween party, he'd have called them a liar. Pulling on the costume and the big yellow duck feet, he shook his head. If they'd told him that he'd be celebrating his one-week wedding anniversary tomorrow, he wouldn't have believed that, either.

He put the duck head on, then glanced at himself in the full-length mirror on the back of the closet door. ''Oh, damn.''

Reaching into the closet, he grabbed a pair of black jeans and stuffed them into a duffel bag along with his boots. One word from anybody and he'd be out of the costume faster than an old maid out of a cake at a bachelor party.

When Chance waddled downstairs, he stopped short at the sight of Lassiter and Sarah standing in the middle of the kitchen. He didn't look any happier to be in costume than Chance did.

"One word and I swear I'll slug you right in the middle of your duck bill," Lassiter warned. He pointed to the Mickey Mouse head sitting in the middle of the table. "I'm gonna look like a damned fool."

Chance studied the man's black tights, red shorts with big white buttons and huge yellow shoes. "Well, at least you get to wear pants. I have to wear duck feet and have my tail hanging out."

"I see you have a change of clothes with you, too," Lassiter said, his expression grim as he put his Mickey head on and picked up a tote similar to the one Chance carried.

Kristen lost a couple of feathers on the polished tile floor when she tapped the toe of one of her clumpy pink pumps. "Chance—"

"They ain't gonna go changin' as soon as we get there," Sarah said, planting her white-gloved hands on her red-and-white-polka dot hips. "Not if I have anything to do with it."

Chance scratched his leg. "If I start itching any more than I already am, you'll have a hell of a time stopping me."

"Same here," Lassiter grumbled.

Kristen opened the back door. "This is a first, Sarah. They agreed on something."

"Mark this day down in the history books," Sarah said, laughing.

Lassiter harrumphed. "Well, don't count on it happening again."

"Not in this lifetime," Chance agreed as they all filed out of the house.

While she waited for Chance to return with soft drinks, Kristen sat on a bale of straw at the side of the dance

floor. A variety of costumed guests line-danced to a popular Brooks and Dunn song, and it was amusing to see
characters like the Cowardly Lion and Foghorn Leghorn
"scootin' their boots."

When they'd first walked into the abandoned barn,
Kristen had marveled at the condition of the interior. Instead of dirt, polished hardwood covered the floor, and
a bandstand, decorated with corn shocks and bales of
straw, held big amplifiers and state-of-the-art micro-
phones. Steve and Beth had certainly put in a lot of effort
to make the barn a nice place to hold parties.

Just as the music ended, Beth walked over and awk-
wardly lowered herself to sit beside Kristen. Dressed like
a medieval lady of nobility, Chance's sister wore a bur-
gundy velvet, high-bodiced dress. It was the perfect costume for a woman in the advanced stages of pregnancy.
"Having fun?" she asked.

Kristen laughed. "I never dreamed how much fun it
would be to see the Tasmanian Devil do the two-step
with a belly dancer."

"That was a sight, wasn't it?" Beth grinned. "Taz
had no idea where to put his hands without touching
skin."

The band started a slow song, and Kristen leaned over
so Beth could hear her. "When Chance talked about a
Halloween party, I thought you'd have it decorated more
like a haunted house."

"We decided it would probably scare the kids, so we
settled on a more general autumn theme," Beth answered, smiling fondly at her husband dancing with Annie. "I see my daughter has found her knight in shining
armor."

The knight, holding Annie, danced his way across to
where Kristen and Beth sat. "Beth, I can't see a thing,"

Steve complained, pushing at his helmet. "This visor won't stay up."

"Does that thing come with a can opener?" Chance asked, walking up to join them.

"If I were you, I wouldn't poke fun," Steve shot back, handing Annie to Beth. "At least my backside is covered."

Kristen accepted the can of soda Chance handed her and bit the inside of her cheek to keep from laughing out loud. Steve's comment to Chance might have been a little more effective if the visor hadn't flopped back down to cover his face.

"I've got a pair of pliers out in the truck," Chance said, thumping Steve's metal chest. "Let's go see if we can fix that thing." He picked up a couple of white feathers from the bale of straw and handed them to Kristen. "I'll be right back, sweetheart. Don't molt too much without me."

Kristen watched the two men head for the double doors. "You don't think they're going to change, do you?"

"Probably," Beth said, her voice distracted as she gazed across the barn at the refreshment table. "Oh, great! Cody's into the cookies again." She set Annie down, then slowly got to her feet. "Come on, sweetie. We'd better stop him before he makes himself sick."

"I bing you a cookie, Ant Kissen," Annie promised.

"Thank you, Annie," Kristen called as the little girl skipped ahead to the refreshment table. She watched the child pick up two large cookies with each hand, then head back across the barn.

"Here, Ant Kissen," Annie said, handing her the chocolate chip cookies before trying to climb the bale of straw to sit beside Kristen.

"Do you mind watching her for a few minutes?" Beth asked on her way across to the bandstand.

"Of course not," Kristen said, helping Annie get settled.

"Thanks."

Kristen munched on one of the cookies and watched Beth thread her way across the dance floor. In a few months, she'd be waddling like that. She polished off the last of the cookie, then dusted her hands of the crumbs. If she didn't stop eating so many sweets, she'd have the waddle long before her pregnancy dictated.

Annie suddenly laughed and clapped her chubby little hands. "Milky Mouse."

"Kristen, let's dance," Mike said, walking up to where they sat on the bale of straw. He shifted from one big yellow shoe to the other. "We need to talk."

"Please, Mike." Kristen rubbed her itching arm as she looked around to see how closely their conversation could be monitored. "Not here."

"Yes, Kristen," Mike said, removing the mouse head. "If I don't do it now..." His voice trailed off.

Taken aback by the strained expression on his face, she glanced down at Annie. "I can't right now, Mike. I'm baby-sitting."

"Go ahead and dance with your dad, sweetheart," Chance said as he approached them. He'd changed out of his costume as had Steve. He gave her a reassuring smile, then picked up Annie to sit on his forearm. "I owe this dance to the munchkin, anyway."

Kristen scratched her leg as she watched Chance waltz out onto the dance floor with his tiny partner before glancing up at the hand Mike extended. She never remembered a time in her life when her father had asked her to dance with him.

"Please, Kristen, will you do me the honor of dancing with me?"

Tears threatened at the sincerity she heard in Mike's voice. Placing her hand in his, she got to her feet and stepped out onto the dance floor.

"Kristen...I..." Mike cleared his throat. "I'm not good at this, but I just want you to know that if you or the baby need anything, all you have to do is pick up the phone." His voice sounded suspiciously gruff. "There's nothing I wouldn't do for you or my grandchild."

Hidden by the Daisy Duck head, Kristen's tears rolled down her face. "Oh, Mike, all I've ever wanted is for you to be proud of me."

Mike couldn't quite blink away all the moisture flooding his eyes. It was the first time in her life she'd ever seen her father shed tears. "I may not be good at letting people know how I feel, but I've always been proud you're my daughter." He cleared his throat before he could go on. "Sarah said it wouldn't kill me to explain things to you. She said you'd understand."

"Understand what?" Kristen asked through her tears. She rubbed at the itch on her stomach. "That you never had time for me? That you always found fault with everything I did?"

"Honey, I..." Mike stopped dancing and led her to the door. Outside, he took her Daisy Duck head off and cupped her face with his hands. His sincere gaze caused hope to rise within her. "When your mother and I married, Sagebrush Boots was on the verge of bankruptcy. It took years of working myself ragged to keep it from going under. By the time I had the company solvent again, your mother had died and too much time had passed. We were strangers. I'd missed most of your childhood, and you weren't interested in getting to know me.''

Kristen sobbed against his shoulder. ''Why didn't you talk to me? Why didn't you tell me?''

He took a deep breath. ''I was afraid you'd reject me. It was easier—safer—to hide my feelings.''

''All these years I…didn't think you loved me.''

A strangled sound rumbled up from her father's chest as he wrapped her in a bear hug. ''Baby, I've loved you from the minute I laid eyes on you in the hospital nursery. I've always loved you and always will. There's nothing that will ever change that.''

''Oh, Daddy, I love you, too.''

Chance watched Kristen move into her father's arms and sway in time to the music. A large rooster and Marilyn Monroe danced past to momentarily block his view. When they moved on, Kristen and Lassiter were nowhere in sight.

''Where the—'' He stopped swaying to look around. ''Annie, did you see where Aunt Kristen went?''

The little girl laid her head on his shoulder, then pointed toward the door. ''Ant Kissen goed ousside wiss Milky Mouse.''

Was Lassiter trying to talk Kristen into leaving with him?

Striding across to Beth and Steve, Chance handed Annie to his brother-in-law. ''I'll have to dance with you another time, munchkin.''

''What's wrong?'' Beth asked. She looked around. ''Where's Kristen?''

Annie yawned and laid her head on her father's shoulder. ''Wiss Milky Mouse.''

Chance nodded. ''Annie said Kristen went outside

with her dad, and I intend to get out there before he talks her into going back to Dallas with him.''

Beth shook her head. ''Chance, he's her father. Surely he wouldn't do or say anything to upset her intentionally.''

Chance didn't even slow down on his way out. ''He'd better not.''

Before he'd taken two steps, Sarah rushed up to him. ''Chance, I think you'd better get out to the parking lot. Kristen isn't feelin' too good.''

Fear, swift and chilling, raced up his spine. Pushing his way through the crowd, Chance broke into a lope as soon as he cleared the door. Standing by his truck, under the glow of a dusk-to-dawn light, Mike Lassiter supported Kristen while she bent to rub both legs.

''What's wrong, sweetheart?'' Chance asked, skidding to a halt at her side.

''I'm…itching…all over.''

She'd taken her Daisy Duck head off, and when she raised her face to look at him, Chance immediately noticed the red blotches on her neck and chin. ''Are you allergic to anything you're aware of, sweetheart?''

''No.'' She pointed to her back. ''Chance, please.''

He scratched where she indicated, then opened the passenger door of his truck. ''Come on, sweetheart. I'm taking you to see a doctor.''

When she started to protest, he put his finger to her lips. ''This isn't negotiable.'' Chance kissed the top of her head. ''Making sure you see a doctor when you're sick is one of those husband things I've been telling you about.'' He grinned. ''It's part of the job description.''

''He's right, Kristen. You need to see a doctor,'' Lassiter said. He touched her cheek, then turned to Chance.

"You'd better take good care of my little girl or hell will be a picnic compared to what I'll do to you, boy."

Chance nodded. "Mr. Lassiter, you don't have a thing to worry about. Kristen will have the best of everything."

Eleven

Chance parked the truck at the side of the house, then shot Kristen an uneasy glance across the cab. She hadn't said more than a handful of words since walking out of Palo Duro Hospital in Canyon. "Sweetheart, what's wrong? You know you can tell me anything."

"It looks like we're off the hook," she said, staring straight ahead.

Apprehension curled in his belly. "What do you mean?"

"I'm not pregnant," she said, her voice shaky.

Chance felt as if he'd been punched in the gut. "But the test—"

"Was wrong." She leaned her head back against the headrest. "The doctor said it doesn't happen often, but once in a while a home test will show a false positive. He did a more advanced test before he gave me the shot for the allergic reaction to the costume."

"Damn!" Disappointment pressed against his chest, but couldn't compare to the fear twisting his gut. Her statement that they were off the hook bothered the hell out of him. She sounded as if there wasn't any reason left for them to stay together. Before he could ask what she'd meant, she opened the truck door, got out and walked into the house.

Sitting alone in the dark cab, Chance gripped the steering wheel with both hands, his knuckles turning white from the pressure. Not having a baby right away wasn't the end of the world, but losing Kristen would be. Only he wasn't sure what else he could do to convince her to stay with him. He'd told her about fate playing a hand in their being together and that their marriage was meant to be. What else could he do?

He watched the light in their bedroom come on. Kristen's silhouette moved across the closed curtains, and he could tell she was changing into her nightgown. He loved that shimmery piece of flimsy silk, but he loved taking it off of her more. Hell, he just plain loved everything about her.

"Well, I'll be damned." The smile, tugging at the corners of his mouth, spread into a wide grin. He'd fallen in love with his wife.

His mood considerably lighter, he got out of the truck and went into the house. He couldn't wait to tell Kristen, to show her with his body how much she meant to him. Surely she'd stay with him after that.

Taking the stairs two at a time, he thought he heard voices behind Lassiter's closed door. Chance grinned. It was probably a good idea that his father-in-law decided to watch a little television before he went to sleep. It would help cover up the sounds of pleasure Chance intended to draw from Kristen when he loved her until they both fell into exhausted sleep.

He entered the bedroom, quickly shed his clothes and climbed into bed. When he reached for her, Kristen turned into his arms without hesitation. Where her cheek rested, tears wet his shoulder and he felt as if a fist had reached into his chest and tried to rip his heart out.

"Sweetheart, it's all right," he said, feeling his own eyes begin to sting.

"Please don't talk," she whispered. "Just make love to me, Chance."

"But I need to tell you—"

Her lips met his, cutting off anything else he was about to say. When she finally let him come up for air, Chance decided the words could wait. He'd show her with his body how much he needed her, how much he wanted her to stay with him, how much he loved her. She was the perfect woman for him, and he fully intended to take all night convincing her he was the only man for her.

Lifting the hem of her silk nightgown, he made quick work of whisking it over her head and tossing it on the floor beside the bed. His hands shook slightly as he filled them with her creamy breasts. He chafed her nipples with his thumbs, then bent to worship them with his mouth. She moaned, ran her fingers through his hair and held him to her, demanding that he draw deeply on the tight nubs.

Kissing his way to her smooth, flat stomach, Chance slid his hand along her side to her hip, then down her slender leg. He trailed his fingers along the inner part of her thigh, teasing the sensitive skin just short of his goal. Her legs moved restlessly and she made soft mewling sounds when he parted her. She was hot, wet and ready for him.

Blood surged through his veins, and he had to grit his teeth against the all-consuming need to bury himself deep inside her. He wanted to take things slow, to love her thoroughly and completely, but Kristen had other ideas. Finding his arousal, she took him into her small hand and stroked him with an urgency that damned near sent him over the edge. She was telling him without words that slow, gentle foreplay wasn't what she wanted. She wanted him now.

Chance gave in to her demands, rolled their protection into place and, with one smooth stroke, joined their bodies. She arched up to meet him and he felt the immediate tightening around him, felt her feminine muscles quiver and caress as her climax overtook her. She gripped his buttocks and tried to pull him closer.

His own explosion close, he withdrew, then surged forward. Kristen met him thrust for thrust, and when he emptied himself, she cried his name as she gave in to the storm a second time.

Chance waited until her shock waves subsided, then moving to her side, gathered her to him. She snuggled close, and almost immediately her breathing became shallow and even as she drifted off to sleep.

He kissed the top of her head and tightened his hold. "I love you so damned much I ache from it, sweetheart," he whispered against her hair. "If you leave me now, there's no way in hell I'll survive."

The minute he opened his eyes, Chance knew Kristen was gone. He reached out for her, but the sheets where she'd lain beside him—loved him throughout the night— were cold. In the week they'd been married, he'd learned one thing about his wife. Kristen wasn't a morning person. No way would she wake up this early unless she had something planned or somewhere to go. The thought sent him vaulting from the bed to find his clothes.

Fear like he'd never known gripped him as he pulled on his boots. On his way downstairs, he stopped by the bedroom Mike had used. To his immense relief the man's luggage sat on the floor where he'd placed it the night he'd arrived.

It wasn't too late. Kristen hadn't taken off to go back to Dallas with her father. At least, not yet.

Feeling as if a weight had been lifted from his shoulders, Chance slowed his pace and headed for the kitchen. But the sound of Mike Lassiter's voice, coming from the study, stopped him dead in his tracks.

"Kristen, I want you to take charge of Sagebrush Boots."

Her gasp of delight sent a chill racing the length of Chance's spine. "I've wanted this for so long, I..."

He didn't wait to hear the rest. He pretty much knew what Kristen would say. She'd dreamed all her adult life of taking over the position her father offered her. She'd trained for it, and as his sole heir, had every right to claim it.

He wandered into his darkroom and turned on the light. The pictures he'd developed the night he and Kristen had returned from Vegas hung around the room. He gazed at the images—pictures of Kristen at the banquet. Even before he'd taken that first drink of champagne he'd been drawn to her and hadn't even realized it.

Swallowing hard around the lump clogging his throat, he turned on his heel, walked to the back porch and grabbed his jeans jacket and hat. Tugging on the jacket, he jammed the Resistol on his head as he pushed through the door and headed for his truck.

Ten minutes later, Chance pulled to a stop on the top

of the ridge overlooking Sundance Valley. It was the very spot where he'd stopped that first day he'd brought Kristen to the ranch. He'd wanted to impress her, to show her that just because he didn't hail from Dallas high society, he for damned sure wasn't a failure. Now the same view caused a cold, painful ache deep inside his chest.

If Kristen left with Lassiter—and he had no doubts she would—what the hell would he do with the rest of his life? At one time, he'd thought the Sundance Ranch and Rodeo Company were more than enough to fulfill him. But that had been before he'd married, and fallen in love with, a fiery redhead with the sweetest kisses and hottest loving a man could ever dream of.

How could he have ever thought her to be the ice maiden?

He'd expected Kristen to be like his mother. After all, they were from the same type of big-city background. But that's where the similarities ended. Julia Warren had always known her family loved her but never appreciated it, was never willing to work at returning their feelings. Kristen, on the other hand, had lived most of her life with doubts and uncertainty about her father's affection. She had depth to her character, whereas Julia was shallow and self-centered.

Kristen was the exact opposite of his mother and everything Chance had ever wanted. She was his woman, his wife, his entire life. So what the hell was he doing sitting on the ridge watching to see when Lassiter took her away?

Chance turned the key in the ignition, jerked the gearshift down into drive and floored it. The truck bounced into potholes deep enough to rattle his teeth as he raced down the road leading into the valley, but Chance just gripped the steering wheel and drove faster. Kristen was his wife. There was no way in hell he'd sit by and lose her without a damned good fight.

Patting his front jeans pocket, his confidence grew. He had his lucky agate. It had never let him down before, and he prayed for all he was worth that it didn't fail now.

By the time he brought the truck to a sliding halt next to the rental car and jumped from the cab, Sarah was helping Lassiter load the trunk.

"I wondered when you'd show up." Lassiter stopped arranging bags to step in front of Chance. "I owe you an explanation."

"Not now. I—"

The older man's hand shot out to grab Chance's arm. "Yes, now. Let's take a walk, son."

Chance raised a brow. "Why should I?"

"Chance, listen to what Mike has to say," Sarah said. The smile she gave Mike Lassiter surprised Chance. If he didn't know better, he'd swear...

"Come on, boy," Lassiter said, turning toward the barns. "You're going to want to hear this."

Chance didn't think so, but he figured he could give the man a few minutes. Kristen wouldn't be going anywhere as long as Lassiter wasn't.

"I've been a fool for a lot of years and it's past time I made this right. Sarah—and seeing you and Kristen together—has made me see that." He cleared the gruffness from his throat. "You never knew it, but your daddy and I were best friends once. We traveled the rodeo circuit together, raised a lot of hell and had a damned good time."

"Sarah told me that much," Chance said, nodding. "But she wouldn't tell me what caused the falling out between the two of you."

The man stopped and took a deep breath. "To make

a long story short, Hank and I both fell in love with your mother, Julia.'' He paused to shake his head. ''That's not right. I only thought I loved her. When she and Hank ran off and got married, I was too stubborn to let it go. I blamed your whole family for my being miserable, when it was my own damned fault. It wasn't Julia, but someone else I really loved.''

Chance frowned. ''Then why did you blame—''

''Pride can be a mighty destructive force, son,'' Lassiter admitted. ''Mine stung something fierce when your mother chose your daddy over me. It was easier to feel betrayed by the both of them and carry a grudge all these years than to admit that I'd been wrong about loving her.''

''But what about your wife?'' Chance asked.

''Martina's fiancé was killed in a plane crash a few months before we met.'' He sadly shook his head. ''She never got over losing him and lost all heart in living. Then, not long after we started seeing each other, she asked me to marry her and take over Sagebrush Boots. She said she couldn't deal with it. And since the woman I loved wouldn't have me because of my pigheaded insistence that Hank had stolen Julia away from me, I agreed.''

''You were probably better off. Dad's life with Mom didn't turn out easy.''

Lassiter nodded. ''I'd heard about her leaving Hank. I'm sorry.''

Chance glanced back at the house. He really didn't want to take a trip down memory lane with Lassiter. He needed to talk to Kristen. ''If that's all you had on your mind—''

''Chance, would you help me carry this to the car?'' Kristen called from the porch.

"No."

Kristen propped her hands on her hips. "Why not?"

"Sweetheart, we need to talk."

Sarah started to interrupt, but Kristen folded her arms beneath her breasts and shook her head. "I'd like to hear what he has to say."

Mike's gray eyes twinkled as he walked over and picked up the bag in front of Kristen. Lowering his voice so only she could hear, he said, "If you have any trouble with that boy, you just give me a call. I'll straighten him out in a hurry."

"I'll do that," she said, careful to keep her voice just as quiet. "I love you, Daddy."

"I love you, too, baby." Mike's cheeks flushed each time he told her he loved her, but Kristen didn't mind. The fact that he truly meant it was all that mattered. "I'll see you in Dallas in a few days." He winked and raised his voice. "I'll go ahead and get this loaded while you two finish your goodbyes."

"Kristen, let's go inside," Chance said, taking her by the hand. The heat of his palm surrounding hers, warmed her all the way to her soul. "I have something I want you to see."

Kristen allowed him to hustle her through the house and into his darkroom. "What do you—"

She stopped short. "My God, Chance, when did you take these pictures?" she asked, moving past him. She walked around the small room gazing at her image on the glossy sheets of paper.

"The night we got married."

"But this was before—"

"Yeah, before the champagne took over." He reached around her to pick up his favorite. "Apparently I had someone at the chapel take this one."

He handed her the photo of them holding a marriage license and his small plume agate. The bride gazed lovingly at the groom. And the groom couldn't have looked happier.

"Why did you enlarge all of them?" Kristen asked, turning to face him.

Stuffing his hands into the hip pockets of his jeans to keep from reaching for her, he shrugged one shoulder. He didn't know how to tell her he'd figured it was all he'd have left of her one day. "Just something to do, I guess."

"Have you ever considered entering your pictures in contests? You're very good."

Chance didn't want to talk about some damned contest or his hobby. "Don't go back to Dallas, Kristen."

"I have to. Mike's retiring next year and I'm taking over Sagebrush Boots."

His heart sank at the triumph he heard in her voice, the look of happiness on her beautiful face. He started for the door. He couldn't ask her to give up her dream, nor could he bear to watch her leave. "I'm sure you'll make a great CEO."

"Where are you going?" she asked, moving to plant herself in his path.

"The Bucket of Suds." Chance started around her. He had every intention of tying on one hell of a bender. Maybe then he wouldn't feel the debilitating ache in his chest, the cold emptiness filling his soul.

Her emerald eyes narrowed and she grabbed his arm. "You're not going anywhere. Not until we get a few things straight. You promised me something and I'm not leaving without it."

Chance ran his hand over his face. God, he'd never realized he could hurt so bad. "Look, Kristen, I don't know what you want from me, but if I promised you something, it's yours. Whatever it is, just take it.''

She reached for his belt. ''Okay.''

''What the hell—'' his voice cracked and he took hold of her hands to stop her, but she pulled away from him and tugged his shirt from his waistband ''—do you think you're doing, woman?''

''I'm going after what you promised me.''

Hope began to surface. ''And you think you're going to find it in my jeans?''

''Well, that's where it starts.''

Giving in to the urge to take her into his arms, he pulled her to him. ''What exactly was it I promised you?''

He'd have given anything to take a picture of the grin she flashed him. ''A baby.'' She wrapped her arms around his waist, then kissed the skin exposed at his open shirt collar. ''And I'm not going anywhere until you give me one.''

He gazed down at her. ''If I give you a baby, sweetheart, we'll have to stay married for a long time. You'll have to stick around through the pregnancy, then another twenty years or so while we raise him.'' Her fingers tickled his ribs. Laughing, he conceded, ''Or her.''

''Nope.'' Her playful expression told him she had something much longer in mind. ''There's the grandchildren and great-grandchildren to consider, Mr. Warren.''

He kissed the tip of her nose. ''That's about fifty or sixty years, Mrs. Warren.''

She nodded. ''At the very least.''

No longer able to keep the playful banter going, Chance hugged her close. ''God, Kristen, you scared me to death. I thought you were leaving me.''

She held him just as tightly. "I don't have to be in Dallas until next week to work out some details before I start my new position."

"Really?" Leaving the Sundance would be one of the hardest things he'd ever have to do. "Sweetheart, I'm not the city boy type. But if moving to Dallas means living the rest of my life with you, then I'll learn to live in the city."

"Don't frown." She smiled and reached up to rub the line from his forehead. "Someone told me once that it causes wrinkles." Her next statement made him grin. "I told my father I wouldn't take over Sagebrush unless I could run the company from here. With on-line computers, faxes and periodic trips to Dallas, I shouldn't have any problems." Before he could tell her how happy her statement made him, she added, "Oh, by the way, Sarah quit this morning."

It took a moment for him to realize what she'd said. "Sarah did what?"

Kristen laughed. "I had to lend her my luggage so she could take off with Mike."

"Where are they headed?"

"To the Little Chapel of the Bells in Las Vegas."

Dumbfounded, Chance stared down at her. He hadn't seen that one coming. "Well, I'll be damned. Sarah's the one your dad's loved for over thirty-five years?"

Kristen nodded and snuggled against him. "He told me the whole story. Apparently she's the love of his life."

"And you're the love of mine." When she pulled back to look up at him, he felt as if he was the luckiest man alive. Digging in his front pocket, he pulled a small velvet box from his jeans. "I've had these since our trip to the mall the other night. But I was waiting for the perfect time to give yours to you.'' He opened the box to show her the matching gold wedding bands. ''Will you stay with me and be my wife by choice, not by accident?''

Tears filled her eyes and a tremulous smile curved her sensuous lips. She stuck out her left hand for him to slip the ring on her finger. ''I love you, Chance. Yes, I'll be your wife for now and always.''

He waited until she'd taken his ring from the case and slipped it on his finger before he pulled her against him. Holding her close, he felt as if their hearts beat as one. ''And I love you, sweetheart. More than life itself.''

She suddenly stepped back and went to work on loosening his belt again. ''Are you going to give me what I want?''

''Depends. I seem to have forgotten what it is,'' he teased.

''A baby.''

Chance laughed. ''Sweetheart, it'll be my pleasure to give you all the babies you want.''

''Good answer.'' The look she gave him made his knees wobble. ''Darling, you are about to get so-o-o-o lucky. Think you can handle it?''

Swinging Kristen up into his arms, Chance headed for the stairs. ''Cowboy up.''

*　*　*　*　*

SILHOUETTE'S 20ᵀᴴ ANNIVERSARY CONTEST
OFFICIAL RULES
NO PURCHASE NECESSARY TO ENTER

1. To enter, follow directions published in the offer to which you are responding. Contest begins 1/1/00 and ends on 8/24/00 (the "Promotion Period"). Method of entry may vary. Mailed entries must be postmarked by 8/24/00, and received by 8/31/00.

2. During the Promotion Period, the Contest may be presented via the Internet. Entry via the Internet may be restricted to residents of certain geographic areas that are disclosed on the Web site. To enter via the Internet, if you are a resident of a geographic area in which Internet entry is permissible, follow the directions displayed on-line, including typing your essay of 100 words or fewer telling us "Where In The World Your Love Will Come Alive." On-line entries must be received by 11:59 p.m. Eastern Standard time on 8/24/00. Limit one e-mail entry per person, household and e-mail address per day, per presentation. If you are a resident of a geographic area in which entry via the Internet is permissible, you may, in lieu of submitting an entry on-line, enter by mail, by hand-printing your name, address, telephone number and contest number/name on an 8"x 11" plain piece of paper and telling us in 100 words or fewer "Where In The World Your Love Will Come Alive," and mailing via first-class mail to: Silhouette 20ᵗʰ Anniversary Contest, (in the U.S.) P.O. Box 9069, Buffalo, NY 14269-9069; (In Canada) P.O. Box 637, Fort Erie, Ontario, Canada L2A 5X3. Limit one 8"x 11" mailed entry per person, household and e-mail address per day. On-line and/or 8"x 11" mailed entries received from persons residing in geographic areas in which Internet entry is not permissible will be disqualified. No liability is assumed for lost, late, incomplete, inaccurate, nondelivered or misdirected mail, or misdirected e-mail, for technical, hardware or software failures of any kind, lost or unavailable network connection, or failed, incomplete, garbled or delayed computer transmission or any human error which may occur in the receipt or processing of the entries in the contest.

3. Essays will be judged by a panel of members of the Silhouette editorial and marketing staff based on the following criteria:

   Sincerity (believability, credibility)—50%

   Originality (freshness, creativity)—30%

   Aptness (appropriateness to contest ideas)—20%

   Purchase or acceptance of a product offer does not improve your chances of winning. In the event of a tie, duplicate prizes will be awarded.

4. All entries become the property of Harlequin Enterprises Ltd., and will not be returned. Winner will be determined no later than 10/31/00 and will be notified by mail. Grand Prize winner will be required to sign and return Affidavit of Eligibility within 15 days of receipt of notification. Noncompliance within the time period may result in disqualification and an alternative winner may be selected. All municipal, provincial, federal, state and local laws and regulations apply. Contest open only to residents of the U.S. and Canada who are 18 years of age or older, and is void wherever prohibited by law. Internet entry is restricted solely to residents of those geographical areas in which Internet entry is permissible. Employees of Torstar Corp., their affiliates, agents and members of their immediate families are not eligible. Taxes on the prizes are the sole responsibility of winners. Entry and acceptance of any prize offered constitutes permission to use winner's name, photograph or other likeness for the purposes of advertising, trade and promotion on behalf of Torstar Corp. without further compensation to the winner, unless prohibited by law. Torstar Corp. and D.L. Blair, Inc., their parents, affiliates and subsidiaries, are not responsible for errors in printing or electronic presentation of contest or entries. In the event of printing or other errors which may result in unintended prize values or duplication of prizes, all affected contest materials or entries shall be null and void. If for any reason the Internet portion of the contest is not capable of running as planned, including infection by computer virus, bugs, tampering, unauthorized intervention, fraud, technical failures, or any other causes beyond the control of Torstar Corp. which corrupt or affect the administration, secrecy, fairness, integrity or proper conduct of the contest, Torstar Corp. reserves the right, at its sole discretion, to disqualify any individual who tampers with the entry process and to cancel, terminate, modify or suspend the contest or the Internet portion thereof. In the event of a dispute regarding an on-line entry, the entry will be deemed submitted by the authorized holder of the e-mail account submitted at the time of entry. Authorized account holder is defined as the natural person who is assigned to an e-mail address by an Internet access provider, on-line service provider or other organization that is responsible for arranging e-mail address for the domain associated with the submitted e-mail address.

5. Prizes: Grand Prize—a $10,000 vacation to anywhere in the world. Travelers (at least one must be 18 years of age or older) or parent or guardian if one traveler is a minor, must sign and return a Release of Liability prior to departure. Travel must be completed by December 31, 2001, and is subject to space and accommodations availability. Two hundred (200) Second Prizes—a two-book limited edition autographed collector set from one of the Silhouette Anniversary authors: Nora Roberts, Diana Palmer, Linda Howard or Annette Broadrick (value $10.00 each set). All prizes are valued in U.S. dollars.

6. For a list of winners (available after 10/31/00), send a self-addressed, stamped envelope to: Harlequin Silhouette 20ᵗʰ Anniversary Winners, P.O. Box 4200, Blair, NE 68009-4200.

Contest sponsored by Torstar Corp., P.O. Box 9042, Buffalo, NY 14269-9042.